Rogue Artists

Rogue Artists

AN ORIGINS ANTHOLOGY

MARIE BILODEAU · R. L. KING
DONALD J. BINGLE · DANIEL MYERS
JENNIFER BROZEK · CAT RAMBO
C. S. E. COONEY · AARON ROSENBERG
SARAH HANS · TRACY R. ROSS
CARLOS HERNANDEZ · JASON SANFORD
CHRIS A. JACKSON · MICHAEL R. UNDERWOOD
ADDIE J. KING · GREGORY A. WILSON

EDITED BY E.D.E. BELL

Rogue Artists

Cover illustration "Unbound" by Charles Urbach
(originally designed for *Noble Treachery* by Great Northern Games)

Published by Atthis Arts, LLC
Detroit, Michigan
atthisarts.com

ISBN 978-1-945009-88-4

Content notes are listed in the back of the collection.

Contents

Art Holds Our Broken Hearts Together

Cat Rambo

A HANDFUL OF MY FAMILY and I were in the last wave to leave the planet.

We clustered around my cousin, who held out their pad so we could see the ship's jerky feed from a rear camera.

Everyone was so quiet you'd think they weren't breathing, jostling side by side. We watched the Pipperi missiles hitting. The globe lit with a flower of fire, the first one in northern Thool, then two burst out on either coast of the emirates, then more and more, until all its surface was lacework of red and gold.

Those impacts hit me in my gut, way down low. I'd always wanted to go out into space, but it was so costly. Someone like me could never afford it. Dreams, only.

Now here I was, on the government's coin, and all I could do was focus on not throwing up on anyone, rather than looking at the stars. People around me trying to hold still but there, breathing out little gasps whenever a favorite part of the world died.

They hadn't let us bring our pets. I'd begged and pleaded for the bakha that I'd raised from a wriggling spraggling, and my parents said no with an exchanged look that I didn't understand until we got to the port and I found out there was only room for me, clutching the carrybag my mother had packed for me and marching forward while they waved goodbye. I only got that one look back over my shoulder, to see their faces, trying to smile at me, trying to smile through their tears.

No one had anything more than that government allotted carry-bag, enough to hold a change of clothes, a few toiletries.

Everyone had stuffed something from home in there. My mother had put in my little stuffed fish, and a packet of play cards my uncle illustrated. Holum, the biology teacher, had cuttings in plastic bags stuffed everywhere, not just in the bag but her pockets. Cleran had their grandmother's prayer robe wrapped around her like a second skin, a little shocking to see something everyone thought so holy exposed like that, but I could understand why she'd not wanted to leave something so precious behind. Gold twined the embroidery's threads, coiling feathers and ferns sprawling thick and lush over the graying fabric.

Sami was my cousin. We'd rescued each other in childhood from one thing or another, but then we'd lost touch after we both got older and went off with our own friends. They brought dyes along with their pad, ones they used in their weaving, made from roots and flowers that no longer existed anywhere else in the whole universe. That thought picked at my soul like someone plucking out bits of it, and not gently.

We all stared at the screen and it showed us the stars, and we had no home beneath our feet. I thought about my bakha, how I'd let it loose out the back door, so it would have those last few hours of freedom before everything turned to fire.

I didn't think about my parents, but I thought about not thinking about them.

The Pipperi didn't shoot the handful of fleeing ships. Most of the vessels rendezvoused at Perim, out at the edges of the solar system, but it was only a matter of time, everyone knew, before the Pipperi came to clean those outer bases away.

Some other species would have to defeat them. We weren't the first, and wouldn't be the last. Our species, which had branded the war in its hubris at first, had learned to its dismay that it was not capable.

And so, with that, we were refugees.

The Volloloy had donated a few planets to housing refugees from the Pipperi but they were packed, and the waiting list was long. Most of us were shipped to Kyuro, but the last groups, mine included, got allotted elsewhere, government after government shifting responsibility, until we ended up on TwiceFar.

———

TwiceFar was a scavenged station, an ancient relic that had been repurposed, and then repurposed again and again, till it housed its own population, serving the ships going back and forth from the nearby gate.

No one seemed to know how long we'd be there, Jerf, who was our appointed leader for going and trying to wrestle information out of the authorities, came back muttering under her breath, "Hurry up and wait, hurry up and wait," and spat whenever anyone asked her what the timeline was.

Rumor had it that much of the station's population were refugees who'd been assigned there and never gotten off. That was the uncertain thing.

I kept walking around trying to think what would it be like if this were our new home. The biology teacher took out her cuttings and made temporary homes for them in cups of water. She even traded a few leaves to the stations' gardeners. There was a lively trade business for those that had managed to bring small, precious things, or even things that were unique because they were made of hard to find materials, like wood or shell or bone.

Sami traded a little flute for credits, but refused to spend them, tucked them away in a pouch. Others were more profligate, usually buying stuff to flavor the daily meals, bars of food of an unvarying and unpleasant consistency and no flavor whatsoever.

———

Two days after we got there, Malia and Lydia, sisters, committed suicide. We knew it wasn't an accident with the airlock, because they left a video saying goodbye. Then they went into the airlock and set it to open so they could step out into space.

I saw the video. It was short. First Malia saying, "I just don't see any point to continuing," and then Lydia saying, "I have to go where my sister goes, there's no choice."

I hadn't known them but Sami had, had been in schooling with them. Not good friends, but better than acquaintances. The news hit them hard, deepened the shadows under their eyes. For the first time they gave up on their appearance, stopped brushing their hair and teeth, and appearing sometimes throughout the day with sleep crust still on their face.

To cheer them up, I talked Sami into going exploring with me. It wasn't exactly forbidden, but it wasn't encouraged. But Sami and I had both found that a lot of people let us capitalize on our youth. They thought it was a shame we were here, and so station folk would look the other way sometimes.

Sometimes not. We certainly got chased out of places that we shouldn't have been in, more than once. An elevator control center whose overseer had stepped down the corridor to investigate mysterious noises, not realizing they were a rattletoy that Sami had set bumping against the wall.

A storage chamber full of cargo going from one place to another. We didn't fiddle much with things, but we did open up one of the smaller crates, and found it full of bricks of some sour yellow paste, sour to the point of inedibility, else we might have stashed some away, desperate for some alteration in our ship rations.

We never got to where the station's brain was stored, but we got to that deck, reaching the transgression that finally pushed the ship authorities' patience past its limits. Uncaring, we were hauled back to the group and scolded multiple times, since every adult, it seemed, felt the need.

After that we stuck to our own deck. Even there, there were plenty of disused spaces, empty holds and vacant suites. TwiceFar was enormous, this version built for a population whose numbers actually had never reached expectations for one reason, then another, which was why it was currently a refugee processing center.

There was a vast cargo hold near us on this deck, totally bare. It was cold in there, bone-chillingly cold, and the walls were metal painted white, the only color the station paint came in.

Still, I said to Sami as we walked through it, "This is big enough that we could all live here."

"That'd explain why it has atmo," Sami said. They tilted their head back, contemplating the ceiling so far overhead for three long breaths. "Yeah, maybe," they finally said. "I don't know how we make it home, though."

We'd seen other holds like this converted into living quarters, so I know they weren't hesitating about the material possibility of it, but rather the people-side.

The unspoken question was, would everyone be willing to do that? Some kept insisting that someday the Pipperi would be defeated, the planet would be inhabitable again. Others wanted to club together on some money-making scheme, get enough to give some of us buy-in to a colony planet. Then they'd work to bring the rest in. A few people just walked around poo-pooing ideas without ever proposing any of their own.

I said, "Maybe we go back and suss out how people feel about it."

Sami half-laughed, half-sneered. They were as unhappy as I was, shredded and raw and not yet able to see a future. "With what, a poll? A survey?"

I looked around at the walls. I waited as long as they had to answer. I said, into the silence, "It's something at least."

"Breathing is something."

"It's the least effort anyone can make."

"Not the least," Sami said, abruptly as a knife's edge. Malia and Lydia, the idea of them out there in space dying before the station's salvage nets caught them, hung between us.

I could see they were thinking about it. I said, "I'd miss you, you know," quietly and they made a sound in answer, not yes, not no, almost a grumble.

But when we got back, there was no need for polls or surveys. Word had come that we were to be relocated again, but this time for good, to a colony that had recently suffered plague and needed new bodies, new hands.

Someone dug out spices from their carrybag and spent them with lavish generosity, let everyone sprinkle a little on their food bars, the illusion of food.

I closed my eyes and chewed more slowly than I ever had in my life, letting the bar soften in my mouth, tasting the two little seeds that had come with the spice, feeling their shape with my tongue before I positioned them, one, then the other, between two teeth and bit down, tasting pepper and sweet, a smell that swelled out through my mouth and nose, a smell that took me for the moment, vividly, viscerally, to a home that no longer existed.

——

The next few days were less quarrelsome, more serene than any had been before. How could they not be? Food tasted better because hope seasoned our tongues. It lightened our steps. Buoyed us up like stepping from heavy gravity to light, that happy upsurge.

It lasted two and a half days, that happiness.

Who knows why the clerk had overbooked colonists? But we were lowest on the list, and the message came with the implication that we would always be lowest on the list. Vestiges of our hubris. Our species wielded power no longer; we had no holdings other than what we had stuffed in our carry-bags, and the clothing on our backs.

That was the lowest moment of the journey for me. For a lot of us.

I said to Sami, bitterly, "We will be here forever."

Sami said, "It will be all right."

I turned away, as I never had from them. I turned away as though I could not hear them.

Sami said, softly, persuasively, "I have thought of a way to spend my credits."

But I didn't care. I kept looking away.

After a while they left and it was then that I let myself cry.

How many hours later was it that Sami came to find me, curled on my cot? It must have been many, maybe even half a day. They said, "Come with me."

"I'm not hungry," I said. "I'm tired. Too tired to move."

They flicked the blanket off me, and I sat up, despite myself, indignant. They stood staring at me, with the blanket in their hand, and I tried to muster up anger, but there was something about the quirk of their lips and then before I knew it, we were both laughing.

"Come with me," Sami said again. They held out their hand and this time I took it and let them pull me up.

"I traded my credits for paint," they said, and tugged me by along until we were at the hold again.

But no longer white. Sami had used their dyes to tint the ship's paint. They'd painted the walls.

With pictures. With our towers, and the trees that had lined our street. With my bakha running free. The peppers that grew in everyone's gardens, and the sky at night and the sky at dawn. The leaves and little insects and the people, so many of them. Even Malia and Lydia walking together, hand in hand.

Everyone was there, they'd crowded in after us. How they'd known to come, I couldn't guess, other than Sami had told them to. Everyone went around from wall to wall, looking at the pictures.

Sami shifted beside me, and I said, "Why?"

"I thought about making a home," they said. "And I started it by making art."

Someone started a praise-song, over in the corner, and Cleran was dancing, holding out the edges of her grandmother's robe, dancing the way our people always had. I knew then that we would stay between the stars, but I also knew that we were home.

I could hear them singing, and I could feel a little of my sorrow seep away as I looked at my bakha, running on the wall, always free, always there.

We make our homes as we make our art as we make meaning out of our lives.

Cat Rambo's 250+ fiction publications include stories in *Asimov's*, *Clarkesworld Magazine*, and *The Magazine of Fantasy and Science Fiction*. In 2020 they won the Nebula Award for fantasy novelette *Carpe Glitter*. They are a former two-term President of the Science Fiction and Fantasy Writers of America (SFWA). Their most recent works are space opera *You Sexy Thing* (Tor Macmillan) and an anthology, *The Reinvented Heart* (Arc Manor, March, 2022), co-edited with Jennifer Brozek.

Catharsis

C. S. E. COONEY

LAST NIGHT, there was a priest at the box office. Not doing anything. Not standing in line. Not even standing across the line, at the other side of the picket, ringing a bell, proclaiming the wrath of la Diosa, wearing one of those daunting tabards embroidered with the two swords: one short, one long (silver and gold for the two moons, Plata the little moon, Oro the big moon), and glaring. No, this priest was just standing there. Arms folded. Still face. Plain clothes. But you can always tell a priest by her tattoos, and the two enameled hairpins that double as throwing knives when loosened from the plaited knots.

Her presence was enough to thin the line in front of the warehouse-turned-theatre. But not all Espadans fear the priests of la Familia de la Diosa these days. Some of the queue scowled openly at her. Others drew up hoods or pulled hats lower, or loosened their hair so that it fell like lace over their faces.

But the priest said nothing, wrote nothing down. Just watched. After I admitted the last person in my line, I collected my money box and went in after them, shutting the door and locking it.

Locked eyes with her first, though. Couldn't read a thing in the priest's stone-still features. Distracted maybe, by her tattoos: the right side of her face split with a vertical golden slash, the left side with a shorter silver one. They marked her as an interrogator.

Maybe she nodded at me, a little? I closed the door too fast to be sure.

Last year, when the queen made her abrupt volte-face regarding her "one nation, one goddess" policy, we were all too shocked and weary to trust it. After all, who changes their mind in a night? And what was to stop her from changing it back? Pass all those old laws anew, insisting that we worship according to her decree or be tried as heretics. No, release from that fear is not an overnight endeavor.

But months passed. The number of priests policing our streets began evaporating like fog at sunny noon. Something inside us began to thaw. And by us, I mean the atheists, agnostics, and religious minorities of Espada. And us actors, of course. Actors may worship all kinds of gods, or none at all, but even the saint-sworn, icon-wearing, sacred-well-sipping Goddess-lovers among us still risked arrest—merely for existing. Because, see, we were actors, and the priests of la Familia had it out for us.

At least now they had it out for us without the benefit of the queen's explicit endorsement. From what I could tell, the religious of la Familia expressed a range of reactions to that change: from relief to chagrin to livid-with-the-bruise-of-rage. But despite the crushing pressures brought to bear upon her from some pretty mighty folks in some pretty holy mantles, the queen was still showing no sign of returning to her previous leanings. It was an improvement, I thought. While it lasted.

It wasn't till a few months ago, when the public gallows were finally broken down in la Plaza de la Fe, and the coal circles swept clean, and the various mutilated effigies buried in the midden, that Yasmin judged it safe enough to bring Teatro Milagro back to the surface. We'd been operating in secret, in cellars and sewers, for several years by then. Underground street theatre, you know? But even before our profession was criminalized, we were by no means high society performance artists.

———

I myself caught the theatre bug when a raggedy troupe of traveling actors stopped by our little farming village with their puppets and masks. I was four years old, Mamá and Papá said, and I kept pointing to the painted wagons and insisting, "I want to live there."

Yasmin had been a theatre professor. Not here, of course; Espadan universities did not offer degrees in the arts. She came to Espada when our troubles began, believing that trouble was the true time for theatre. She set up her workshop in the slums. She could have lived in a much nicer neighborhood—with linden trees and paving stones and actual gutters—but I'm glad she didn't. The slums are where I met her: me, busking on the streets with a few friends, doing one of our song-story cycles for petty change.

Song-stories. For lack of a better word (and there was one, Yasmin assured us later, though, to be fair, when translated out of its original language, it pretty much still meant "song-stories"), that's what we called the old ballads we'd repurposed into one unified narrative line. We threaded them together with patter and dialogue, differentiating the multiple characters we each played by moving into exaggerated postures, modulating our voices, and suggesting costume changes: a red ribbon, a white glove, a black domino, a blue girdle, a skeleton key. Yasmin stood across the street watching us till we'd run through the cycle three times—a good two hours—then came over and started asking questions. She also made a few suggestions.

Some of us took instant umbrage. But some of us (me) recognized *her* thing as the thing that would make *our* thing better. There were words for all these things, but I didn't know them at the time: director, devisor, the outside eye. Yasmin was the element I didn't know we'd been missing.

Since then, we'd diverged and diversified as a troupe. But always it was me and Yasmin at the center, improvising and codifying, composing and improving. When things got really bad in Espada, when the coal circles smoldered day and night, and the gallows ropes creaked even when no wind blew, Yasmin and I—and, eventually, Xime and Alejandra and Luz and Amir and Guillermo and Xavier—went underground and rehearsed our latest works in the dark.

"When shit goes down, we go up," said Yasmin, but she meant artistically, not literally. Although sometimes we rehearsed in attics too, when we could borrow one.

Teatro Milagro, we were now calling ourselves, after cycling through as many names as auxiliary ensemble members. We were in the mood for miracles. The big one especially: that once turned, the queen's mind would not turn back.

About that. Last year, round about the time she granted her first general pardon to all prisoners convicted on charges of heresy, gossip was just starting to circulate about a royal marriage. Could be that's what did it. Not all countries believe as the Espadan majority does; it would look strange to go and marry someone who believes in something you've made a crime on your own streets. Our neighbors to the east worship something they call "las voces de las estrellas," a collective entity of immortals that views us humans as embryonic consciousnesses. Or, as an ex-lover (an easterner of Milfuegos, the greatest metropolis of Primavera) once explained, "as barely sentient bread dough." The islanders of Mariposas to the south don't so much worship as befriend the "little spirits" who live amongst them (la Familia calls them devils), and do not ask me to number the deities of north-most Piedra, because they are legion.

Whatever the source of the miracle—be it economics or expedience—it brought the nationhead of Espada to her senses. At least for now.

And for now, our newly legalized Teatro Milagro meant to put on a show.

—

Yasmin claims to have thought up the name Teatro Milagro, but I remember suggesting it about three weeks before she did, and my idea being dismissed at the time, only later to emerge as her own. Yasmin does not always process "in mud time," as she calls moment-to-moment reality. It takes her a while to digest some new thoughts in full. Often when she does, she's made it wholly her own—no matter the origin.

But that, my friends, is the nature of collaboration. We must remain fluid and flexible. When we cannot anymore, when we come down at last to our own inner steel, we must remember to swing out with the flat end first, not the point.

And really, whenever I remind Yasmin about my part in a project, especially if it's my soul-stuff at the very heart of it, she'll laugh and say, "That's right, Vega; I forgot! We'll put your name down as first among creators," and it's all done so good-naturedly that I enter into our next collaboration with no compunctions.

———

I don't remember which one of us thought up the idea of la Cámara de las Sombras. Not one of mine, or even Yasmin's. I truly think it was one of those group thoughts that seem to form in the air like a new note of music hovering above a harmonizing chorus. Our troupe is so tight-knit now, this happens more often than not. I put it down to all our mask work.

I first noticed this cohesion when we were devising our Los Lobos piece, back when we were still in hiding. The audience would cram in to see us—all word of mouth; we pasted no broadsides in those days—and sit among the root storage or dusty wine bottles, right there on the dirt floor, and watch us actors do nothing but loll about.

But we lolled about as *wolves.*

We wore wolf masks, and did wolf things: hunt lazy beavers, educate our sprightly pups, care for our sick and injured, mourn the passing of our elders. We would pretend that individuals from our audience were tree stumps to be marked, carcasses to be sniffed, or perhaps strange wolves to be howled at. You'd be surprised how often the audience howled back!

Yasmin played the human hunter, come for our pelts. We never knew when she'd arrive, clashing her symbols in a murder of sound. The terror of it. We'd all respond the exact same way, every time: startled, urgent, springing up, bounding away. You cannot rehearse this unity, not exactly. You can only prepare your body, as best you can, to empty itself—to allow the wolf in. When we wear the masks, we become one. Not just with the masks. With each other. A pack.

Some of us weren't quick enough to escape Yasmin the Hunter. The very young wolves, who knew no better. The very old, too stiff to move. But some nights, the weak ones did escape—when the strong wolves stayed to fight. We never knew, in any given performance of Los Lobos, who would survive at the end: the wolves or the hunter. How many wolves would die. How many pelts the hunter would take. If the hunter would return, bleeding and triumphant, to her hut. Or not at all.

———

We were raided once, during a Los Lobos performance. Our last. We lost Xavier that night. The priests took him. Charged him with the usual crimes brought against actors, prostitutes, and bookies: "unseemly exhibitions and extravagant acts of dissipation."

No trial to speak of, but found guilty. Sentenced to a term of "incandescence." This did not necessarily mean execution. Had it been spring or autumn, Xavier might have served his sentence and been released: starved, perhaps, filthy, certainly, and louse-ridden—but alive. But it was high summer. And so, under the leaden roofs of la Diosa's temple palace, Xavier was sweated dead, like so many others.

The priests hung his effigy—wolf mask and all—over the barred doors of the old Royal Theatre in la Plaza de la Fe. Not that Xavier had never played there, nor any of us ever dreamed of it. It was a statement. The hunter would always come for the wolves. Beasts deserved no better.

—

We had no plans to revive the Los Lobos project for Teatro Milagro. We wanted something new, something that ended in a feeling of luminosity, of tenderness. For how, we asked ourselves, could we live in this new light—we actors, yes, but we Espadans too, from the hobgoblinish guttersnipes to the queen herself—if we did not publicly acknowledge and exorcise our cultural darkness, eh?

We made it sound like a haunted house. A lark. Come to la Cámara de las Sombras! Run the gauntlet of your nightmares. Watch as your past sins take shape before your eyes. You will face them. You will move through them, beyond them, and out the other side, into the light. At the end: a feast!

We claimed—publicly, brazenly—that Teatro Milagro would provide what previously only la Diosa could bestow: ritual expiation for anyone brave enough to buy a ticket.

What else was theatre for?

—

It was a hit. Maybe too much of one.

First, the picket line formed outside the warehouse we rented when the workers left for the night. Crowds of protestors, faithful servants of la Diosa, alternating between shouting obscenities at us and interceding with la Diosa (loudly) on behalf of our souls. This behavior spiked the interest of those who'd had no interest in theatre heretofore. Admission numbers—and numbers of picketers—swelled.

Yasmin was excited, almost fierce with it. My stomach was old ropes dissolving in acid. Despite the queen's new policy, Espada was still Espada. We were still actors. Priests were still priests. I remembered Xavier: man, prisoner, martyr, effigy. His wolf mask hung above my bed. I talked to it as I would a ghost.

Last night, after that priest had showed up, I couldn't sleep for worry, no matter how Yasmin grinned.

"Let her fume and glower. Nothing we're doing is illegal. Not anymore."

But of course, it was not *Yasmin* who was working the box office when the priest returned.

This time, she stood in the box office line, patiently awaiting her turn to buy a ticket. It was not long before we were face to face, only a wooden table between us. (To call this table our "box office," when it is not in fact an office nor do we have any box seats to sell, is one of our troupe's many eccentricities. But unabashedly pretending one thing is something else that it patently isn't—even when we don't need to—is a perk of our profession.)

"So," said the priest, plunking down three copper coins onto my table, "how does this work?"

———

When I didn't answer right away, she raised her eyebrows. I blinked up at her. I wished it were Yasmin's turn to work the box office. Gathering my wits, I said, "Audience members enter the vestibule, one at a time. You stand in darkness and speak your crimes. After a few minutes, a curtain will lift. You will walk through it. A guide will meet you and take you through your bespoke experience."

Some people didn't make it past the vestibule. They couldn't bring themselves to speak their sins. (We usually called them "sins," but the word "crimes" slipped out of my mouth just now. It never had before.)

Very few demanded their money back. They just exited the way they entered and walked quickly away.

But those who made it through the vestibule usually stayed for the whole show. They exited out the back of the building, where little pasteles and cups of fruit juice awaited them. They were given washcloths and bowls of water to wipe their sweat and tears away, and a small fabric flower made from scraps of costumes too tattered to repair.

I did not tell the priest any of this. I, personally, did not think she would make it through the vestibule. My best imaginings had her fleeing back through the entrance in shame and fear. My worst imaginings had her stalking through la Cámara de las Sombras, flinging open the back door and letting in the Familia's guard, who would then arrest all the actors in my troupe one by one, and drag them out the back to the prison wagons. And I alone would be left outside, with a growing line in front of me, and a mob of angry picketers howling for my blood, and I would never know what became of my friends.

The priest received the stamp on her hand that acted as her ticket. (Why we call it a ticket instead of a stamp is another mystery of the theatre.) She examined it closely: a red wolf's head. Her mouth did something. She nodded a little. Her shoulders hunched, then straightened. Her eyes locked with mine, as they had done last night, and her chin jerked.

Then she disappeared through the door.

———

I waited. Most experiences in la Cámara de las Sombras lasted about a quarter hour. But it could be longer, if the individual audience member had much to confess.

It was more than fifteen minutes later when I felt a hand on my shoulder.

Yasmin.

"Vega," she said. "I'll take over. We need you for this one."

She slipped a mask into my hand. She also kissed my cheek, lightly. Yasmin's perfume always reminded me of raspberries.

"Strong heart," she wished at me, then sent me inside.

The fact that it had taken the priest so long to confess told me that our forthcoming improv would be an elaborate one. The human imagination is a pageant; a parade of nightmares may take many shapes. The actors of Teatro Milagro, eavesdropping from the other side of the curtain, have only a few moments to prepare from the time a confessor concludes their list of sins to the time they step into la Cámara de las Sombras.

I did not myself know what I was walking into. I did not need to for the role I played. In la Cámara de las Sombras, I only ever played one part.

But I was curious; I liked to see my fellow actors work, so I pulled my mask on and my hood up. This, with my dark clothes, made me effectively invisible. I followed the priest quietly from the shadows, and watched her fears unfold.

Xime and Amir were our main dancers—trained acrobats—who could create instant architectures from their twining limbs. Their bodies could roll and tumble like moving vehicles: royal carriage, cabbage cart, tumbril of the condemned. They leapt through, swung from, and hung from aerial loops dangling from high rigs, each a portal, or a window, or a hell hole (depending on what was needed). Sometimes they were hordes of demons clinging to the hanging silks, swarming and soaring and scuttling with the agility of birds, of monkeys.

Alejandra and Luz were older, less flexible, not as swift, but they carried a gravitas in their bodies that bound the eye fast. In their elastic expressions and deep gazes, the range of human emotion played out: agony, fear, bitterness, desire, appetite, rage, defeat, despair.

Guillermo acted both as guide and sound-maker. The man could produce such noises from his body—percussive, shrill, resonant, flatulent, monstrous—and carried instruments enough to produce an even wider variety. He walked backwards, beckoning the audience onward through the moving scenes, and augmented the elaborate mimes with whatever soundscape he deemed appropriate.

The priest's personal nightmare—so it seemed to me—was her last decade of obedience to religious superiors, while the faith that had once nourished and compelled her was slowly chipped away with every torture, imprisonment, and execution she carried out. The actors did not need to embody every victim, but all victims. The gestalt, Yasmin would say. Five bodies writhing together in a knot became a hundred, a thousand. They reached for succor with desperate arms, and grasping nothing, fell back, clawing at their prison walls, at each other, gasping for breath that was harder and harder to come by.

Huddling into an ever tighter knot, they passed a single, wan candle around. One by one, they tried to keep it alight, even as they themselves flickered out. Fell back into shadow. Until one frightened actor was left. Holding their faltering stub of candle. Standing alone beneath the silks, where four other bodies hung like limp moths in a spiderweb.

The remaining actor—it was Luz—quickly thrust the candle into the priest's startled hands. Then the silks of the gallows seemed to drop down and loop around her like a python, hauling her towards the ceiling, where she, too, dangled, broken.

Which was when I stepped out from behind the priest. Staring up at the dead, she seemed unaware of the hot wax falling into her hand. I was fully in front of her before she knew I was there. She caught just a glimpse of my mask before my hand shot forward, pinching the candle out.

———

I never know what they see, when they see me in the mask.

When I am not wearing it, the mask looks like nothing much: a neutral face, slightly too elongated and too smooth to be quite human, finished in a shining black lacquer. I'd come across the mask in the sewers one evening a few years ago, on my way to one of our forbidden rehearsals. I'd put it on to surprise my troupe.

That didn't work out how I'd thought. Three of them screamed and fled from me. Two burst into tears and babbled like babies. One fainted (Xavier, when he was still with us).

Only Yasmin seemed to know it was me, for she came up quietly and said, in her calm professor's voice, "You're frightening them, Vega. I do not think that is an ordinary mask. It is a very special mask, and you must only wear it for very special performances."

She removed it gently, gingerly, and handed it to me at once, as if it burnt her fingers. But her eyes were radiant with that too-fierce excitement when she said, "I could almost believe in your Goddess, that such a thing fell into our hands."

I do not wear the mask for every performance of la Cámara de las Sombras. Only the ones where Yasmin deems it needful—only at the very end, and only a glimpse. That's all it takes. Any more, and they can break. And a broken audience member cannot come to our next show, can they?

———

The priest had tucked her cloth flower between her two enameled hair pins. Her face yet had a gray pallor to it, and a clammy sheen of sweat, for all that she had scrubbed herself vigorously with the washcloth we handed her. She clutched her cup of juice in one hand, her pastel in the other, but could not bring herself to eat or drink. She sat in the dry yellow grass behind the warehouse, looking out over the river that moved murky and slow through this industrial area of the city.

I sat down beside her, cross-legged. She flinched slightly, as if I were still wearing the mask. They always know, somehow, that it was me, after. Even when I remove the mask and put it away in our box of props with all the others, and am just Vega, in my homespun clothes, with my plain peasant's face.

"How are you feeling?" I asked her.

Her lips twisted. "How am I supposed to be feeling?"

I shrugged.

"Is that it?" she demanded. "Am I clean now? Is all forgiven?"

I rested my chin on my shoulder and regarded her. "What do you think?"

"I think . . ." She drew a deep breath. "I think my mouth tastes like vomit. And I may have shit myself."

"That's normal. It's why we have a privy set up back here." I indicated the cup in her hand. "The juice will help. Try it."

She glanced warily at her drink, then downed it. Shuddered at the sweetness. Some color returned to her face.

"Is there a word for it? What just happened?"

There was. Yasmin had taught it to me. It meant puking and shitting, yes. It also meant the other thing. The thing that was making the priest's hands tremble even now, that pressed like a warm palm to the center of her back, loosening her shoulders. That made her expression as wide-open as a child's, whereas before it was a stone wall.

I smiled at her, full as tired as she, and as full of wonder. Then I looked out again over the river.

After a moment, the priest broke her pastel into two pieces, and handed me one. We chewed together in silence, in the dark.

C. S. E. Cooney lives in Queens, New York. She won the World Fantasy Award for her collection *Bone Swans* in 2016. Her new collection, *Dark Breakers*, featuring stories set in the same world as *Desdemona and the Deep* (Tor.com, 2019), came out from Mythic Delirium in February 2022. Her novel *Saint Death's Daughter* debuted with Solaris in April 2022. Currently, she and her husband, author Carlos Hernandez, are co-developing a TTRPG about "Inquisition and Aliens" called Negocios Infernales, forthcoming from Outland Entertainment.

ARTBOT

Sarah Hans

Amina's belongings were delivered ten days after her death. Her mother Iris was called to the cargo bay to collect the crates, and she stood staring at them for a long time, so long the cargomaster cleared his throat at least three times.

"I'll need you to sign for them," he said gruffly, presenting her with a tablet awaiting the press of her index finger.

Iris looped her thumbs in her tool belt and shook her head. She thought of her tiny apartment in the Blue sector, which was the size of a closet, with three flights of stairs to reach it. She gestured at the crates. "Where would I put all this?"

The cargomaster shrugged and again presented the tablet. "There's storage rental in Red sector."

Iris couldn't afford storage rental anywhere, especially not in Red sector. She imagined telling the cargomaster to stick his tablet somewhere rude, but the thought of Amina's belongings being auctioned off to strangers or sent to the trash compactors made her stomach clench. She hadn't seen her daughter in nearly ten years, and they hadn't parted on the best terms. This was all she had left of Amina.

So Iris pressed her index finger to the tablet and headed to Red sector, the cargobots following behind her with the crates. Storage would cost nearly a month's wages. She pressed her finger to another tablet to authorize that transaction, knowing she couldn't afford anything past that one month. She'd have to sort through what she could and decide what to do with it all before the second payment.

She wanted more time, but that was literally a luxury she couldn't afford.

After a sweaty day's labor in the engine rooms under Green sector, Iris brought her aching body to the storage unit the next day. The crates were the cheapest available, cheap plastic easily dented and warped, and she had to use a screwdriver to pry off the lids. Inside, the items were a mad jumble, packed hastily and without care. Many items were broken, but honestly, they may have started that way.

Looking down at her child's belongings, Iris recalled their last argument. Amina had worked for years to save the money she needed for transport to some artist collective on a trash planet light years from home. Iris had tried to convince her it was a waste. "What will you do on a trash planet? There are no jobs there, no opportunities."

Amina had rolled her eyes in that infuriating way she had. "That's the point, Mum. I don't want to be a pilot or a mechanic or a waste-treatment specialist."

"This station is the largest in this quadrant. There are more careers on offer than just those," Iris had told her.

"I don't want to live this life," Amina had said, gesturing around their small apartment with a frown. "I don't want to scrape and struggle every day, one day's wages away from becoming indentured to the station. I don't want to contribute to this wasteful system anymore. I want to be part of the solution."

Iris had been so hurt. She couldn't help taking it personally when her daughter spoke like their life, the life Iris had worked so hard to build, the life that had given Amina so much, was so worthy of scorn. "If this life, *my* life, is so repulsive to you, then maybe you should go. Maybe you should see what it's like somewhere else, somewhere without doc-bots and food printers and environmental controls."

Amina had been right, of course, in many ways. Living on the space station was hard. Everyone living and working here ended up indentured to the company as prices always seemed to rise conveniently higher than wages. But Iris failed to see how anywhere else was better, and certainly not a trash planet.

She had expected her daughter to call her for a ticket home within a few months. But she hadn't. Amina had always been stubborn. For ten years, the two of them didn't speak, Iris waiting for the call wherein her child admitted defeat, and Amina, her mother assumed, too proud to ask for help of any kind.

Now, looking in the crates that comprised all her daughter's worldly goods, Iris wondered if maybe Amina had successfully created a life for herself in that artist collective. In the first crate, the top layer was made up of mismatched utensils, multicolored pottery, trinkets and jewelry made from sparkling bits of glass—everything constructed from patchworks of other broken items Amina must have found in the copious refuse on her new home planet. At the bottom, Iris found blankets put together from pieces that must have been cut from other, larger blankets, no doubt ruined, Amina saving each piece so she could sew them all together with sparkling thread.

Iris pulled a blanket from the crate and sat on the floor, pressing the fabric to her nose before she could stop herself, hoping to catch the scent of Amina's skin lingering on the threads. It smelled musty.

Beep.

Iris started and looked around the storage unit.

Beep.

She dropped the blanket, got to her feet, and inspected the crates.

Beep.

The sound was coming from the third crate, pushed up against the wall. Iris fetched the crowbar and pried open the lid, the beeping a steady soundtrack to her efforts. Inside, the crate appeared to be full of rugs woven together out of colorful, mismatched fabrics.

Beep.

Iris knelt and yanked at the top layer of rugs. Beneath them, a red light glowed. She cleared rugs away until she could see the source of the noise and light: a tangle of metal limbs curled in on themselves like the legs of a dead spider. She reached in and tried to lift it out, but it was heavy, a thick base hidden beneath the many legs. When she pulled her hand back, her hand met with something sharp and drew blood. On closer inspection, she had been cut by a pair of scissors welded to one of the legs. All the legs had tools welded to them, in fact, except for two, which had grabby pincers.

Beep.

The side of the crate provided considerably more resistance than the top, and Iris's wrists throbbed by the time she pried it off. Handwoven rugs tumbled onto the floor, revealing the robot nestled inside. On the base, scribbled in Amina's beautiful, chaotic handwriting, pink letters declared this to be ARTBOT.

Iris swallowed the sob that unexpectedly rose to her throat. She busied herself inspecting the robot further. There was no switch she could find to activate it, but she found a battery compartment, and an old-school charging cable coiled in a clever nook. The beeping and red light were probably low-power indicators. She uncoiled the charging cable and plugged it into the wall, smiling to herself at the kismet. A newer, more expensive storage unit wouldn't have this type of old-school charging plate, but it was a perfect match for Amina's robot. Like it was meant to be.

The beeping stopped and the red light flashed a steady rhythm, which Iris assumed must mean the robot was charging. She stood back from the crate and smiled a little. Amina had always been mechanically inclined, like her mother, but had eschewed mechanics in favor of art. Iris had told her many times mechanical engineering could be just as beautiful and meaningful as creating art. Repairing engines and constructing replacement parts for old ventilation systems required creative thinking, and it was deeply satisfying work, especially because she knew she was actively helping people survive on the space station. She was doing critical tasks. She might not be paid like it, but she was important to the continued success of the whole community.

And Amina had finally discovered some small part of her mother's joy when she made this robot.

Iris slept well that night, better than she had since she learned of Amina's death.

———

A crisis in Yellow sector took all of Iris's time for the following three days. She slept for fourteen hours when it was over, and finally returned to the storage unit feeling rested but aching. She stopped at the street vendor near the storage unit for a taco, and when the storage unit door swung open on creaking chains, she dropped her taco on the floor.

The second crate had been opened. Beside it, something had been constructed, probably from whatever had been inside. Bits of glass and metal had been fused together. Fabric had been cut, sewn, and draped. Paint had been applied. It was a statue, a crude statue. And Iris knew immediately who the statue, with all its sharp angles and glittering details, was supposed to represent.

Amina.

Iris approached the statue cautiously, as if it might come to life. She raised one hand and laid it against the familiar lines of her daughter's face, captured in glass and metal, with brass bolts for eyes and a mosaic of brown shards for lips. The resemblance was uncanny.

Tears flowed down her face, unlocked by the sudden appearance of her daughter's likeness, a patchwork ghost constructed of flotsam. Beside the statue, ARTBOT crouched, legs folded in, tools politely concealed, a green light glowing where the red had been. It had an aura–if a mechanical object could possess an aura–of satisfaction.

"You miss her too, eh?" Iris asked, laying one hand on the robot's base. It gave no indication it understood, but Iris knew it did. She contemplated how she could add an interface so she could communicate with it better. "Sorry, but you're stuck with me now." Her voice cracked and she sniffled, tracing the word written on the robot's base with one shaking finger, remembering how she had once taught Amina how to write her name by holding her hand over her daughter's tiny fingers, directing the pencil, the straight lines and swooping letters.

"What is *that?*" A voice asked from the doorway. The storagemaster stood there in a Red sector jumpsuit with a clipboard, eyes wide, staring at the statue of Amina. "And how did it fit in those crates?"

Iris smiled and dashed her tears away with the sleeve of her own jumpsuit. "It's my daughter's artwork."

"It's incredible. I've never seen its like, and a lot of art moves through this sector. I imagine someone in White sector would pay a year of my wages for it."

Iris gazed up at it again, the harsh light reflecting off Amina's amber glass cheekbones and giving her a sort of glow. The statue was so beautiful, and the resemblance to Amina so perfect, it was hard to look at. "It's not for sale," she said softly.

The storagemaster nodded, as if they understood. "Well if she makes anything else, I know some people who might be interested. There's a gallery in White sector'd probably eat this up. Never seen anything like it."

Iris smiled at the repetition. She'd never seen anything like Amina's artwork before, either, but she'd never been any great connoisseur. She'd never thought it was *truly* unique. But maybe it was. Maybe Amina really had been a gifted artist, even more than her own mother knew.

She ran her fingers carefully across ARTBOT's nearest limb. "Maybe she'll make more for us."

The storagemaster nodded, mumbled something else that sounded appreciative, and backed away, moving down the corridor of storage units until their shuffling steps could no longer be heard.

Iris sighed and patted the robot affectionately. "I've never heard of an artbot before. You might be the first of your kind." She wondered, given a supply of worn-out engine parts and trash from the compactor bins, what else her daughter's creation could construct. Maybe the storagemaster was right, and people would even pay to see it, the first robot artist, Amina's incredible creation. She imagined people crowded around the statue of her daughter, gaping, while ARTBOT worked in a flurry of mismatched metal limbs to construct something new and exciting, another glittering statue made of the space station's discards.

Iris sighed, leaning back against the nearest crate, and pulled one of her daughter's blankets across her lap. Her chest hurt, and she pressed her hand against her sternum. Was it sorrow that finally welled up in her, bringing her this pain?

No, she decided. The emotion was pride.

Sarah Hans is an award-winning writer, editor, and teacher whose stories have appeared in more than 30 publications, including *Love Letters to Poe* and *Pseudopod*. She is the author of the horror novel *Entomophobia* as well as the short story collection *Dead Girls Don't Love*. You can also find her on Twitter, Instagram, and TikTok under the handle @witchwithabook, where she loves to talk about living the spooky life. She lives in Ohio with her partner, stepdaughter, and an entirely reasonable number of pets.

Art In

Aaron Rosenberg

THE SECOND TIME someone tripped over the pothole he'd drawn, Art giggled. The man turned to glare at him but Art just sneered, daring the corporate goon to say anything, to make something of it. Instead, the man huffed and stormed off, deliberately stomping right through the middle of the illusory hole and dragging his heel to scuff the chalk there. Well, whatever. Art had gotten enough entertainment out of it. And the way clouds were massing overhead, all signs of his work would be washed away soon enough, anyway.

Which was totally fine with him. Better, even. He didn't need to create some sort of "permanent art installation" like some of his peers back from school. Nah, for him it was all about the transience, the fleeting nature of the work—and its ability to startle and distract while it existed.

"Why do you waste your time with antics like that?" his uncle Chandran demanded when Art recounted his latest triumph over dinner that night. "You possess real talent, Arvind. Yet all you do with it is these juvenile pranks." The older man shook his head. "Very sad."

"It's Art," Art muttered, but couldn't meet his uncle's eyes despite his bluster. "I'm honing my skills, uncle."

"For what?" Chandran asked him. "For more of these tricks and jokes? They mean nothing, and so they will come to nothing."

He sliced a hand sideways through the air, dismissive. "Garbage in, garbage out."

"Chandran, you are too hard on the boy," his auntie Jayatri admonished, reaching out to pat Art's hand consolingly. "He is still young. He will find his way."

"I hope so," was all his uncle said, but the clear doubt in the statement weighed heavily on Art, settling around his shoulders even after the meal had ended and he had taken himself off to his tiny closet of a room.

There, the walls covered in his scribbled sketches, Art lay back on his bed, arms behind his head, and stared up at the ceiling and the fantastical mosaic he'd drawn there over the years. Was his auntie right? Would he find some ideal, some goal, some direction? Or was his uncle correct, and he would simply drift uselessly forever?

It wasn't that he wanted to be like this. But nothing seemed to matter to him. Not really. Only the art itself. That was valuable and important for its own sake, not for anything or anyone else.

Idly, Art scooped up a pencil and sketched a quick image on the wall just above his headboard. A handful of quick lines formed the borders, then the crossbars, and a few shaded slashes suggested glass panes. A small window. Sunlight beyond it, a pastoral image unlike anything in his neighborhood or experience but real nonetheless. Powerful.

As he finished the image, it took on depth, solidity, the same way he felt his street sketches did. Only this time, it was clearer, more certain. Somehow the glass became slick and smooth, the window frame rough and textured. And the landscape! The sun shone, casting light into the room far beyond what his standing lamp provided. The warmth of it heated Art's face and chest, and he closed his eyes, enjoying the sensation.

Then they popped back open as the truth of that struck him. What the hell?

He studied the sketch, but already the lines were blurring, fading, the rough texture of the wall rejecting the pencil lead, paint winning out. The sunlight dimmed, then was gone, nothing but a vague impression of its earlier warmth remaining.

But he had felt it. It had been real.

Hadn't it?

Hopping up, Art crossed the room—which only took a few steps—to his desk. There he tugged out a sketchbook, flipped to a blank page, and, plopping cross legged onto the messy floor, drew a quick image of a bird. Small, pert, with a sharp little beak and a twinkle in its eye and a splash of color across its chest and down both wings. A songbird—he didn't know the exact type but he'd seen them all around on balconies, lampposts and streetlights.

He added the last bit of shading to the feet and the feathered head—and the bird twitched. It stirred. Then it took a little hop, tilted its head at him, opened its beak, and sang.

Art flopped backward like he'd been shoved, jostling the sketchbook so it slid off his lap and onto the floor, the image facedown. The song continued a second or two longer before trailing off, growing softer until it was entirely gone. When he righted the book, the bird was just a sketch once more.

But he had seen it move. He'd heard it sing.

Somehow, he'd brought the image to life. Even if only for a few seconds.

How?

A soft knock startled him from his thoughts. Scrambling to his feet, Art lunged for the door and yanked it open, to find Auntie Jayatri standing there.

"Are you all right?" she asked. "I thought I heard—" She shook her head, her dark braid whipping behind her. "Music?"

"You did!" Grabbing her hand, Art tugged her into the tiny bedroom, shutting the door behind them both before showing her the sketchbook still in his other hand. "Here. I drew this."

She studied the songbird. "Very nice." Her tone made it clear she did not see the connection.

"Look. Watch." Taking the pad back, Art added another bird above the first.

It sat on the page, unmoving.

Jayatri did watch, and her smile was warm. "You have such wonderful skill," she told him. "Just like your mother." There was a distant look in her eyes as she recalled her dead sister. "Sometimes, when she painted, you felt as if you could hear the ocean or the wind, as if the leaves in the forest were almost moving or the waves shifting." She patted his cheek. "You are much like her, you know. She, too, would lose herself in her art."

She turned to go, and Art let her, torn between thoughts of the mother he barely remembered and frustration at the lifelike but static images on his own page. Why had it not worked this time? What had gone wrong?

Frowning at the sketch, he remembered what his aunt had said. He was sure what he'd seen and felt a few moments ago had been real. Had his mother been able to do the same thing? There were a few of her paintings here in the apartment, and they were lovely, but he'd never felt anything out of the ordinary from them. Perhaps the effect had been equally short-lived? All of those pictures were over a decade old now.

What else had Jayatri said? "Lose yourself in your art." He did. When he drew, there weren't any concerns about salability, about permanence, about how others would react to the image, even about his own feelings toward it. It was the art itself that was important, the act of creation. The image was everything.

Except just now. He'd drawn that second bird to show his aunt what had happened with the first. That had colored the process. Could it have tainted the image itself?

Leaning against the closed door, Art took a deep breath, then another. He closed his eyes and put all thoughts of reality and proof from his mind. That wasn't why he made art. When he felt he had restored his usual level of nonchalance, he drew a third bird on the page, not worrying about anything, letting the art speak through him rather than forcing an interpretation or need upon it.

And this time, as he added the last pencil stroke to the beak, the little songbird rewarded him with a trill of music that filled the room and lifted his soul, much as the sunlight had.

He'd done it! It was real!

The question was, what to do about it?

—

The next day, Art was still tussling with that question. He'd gone to work—his uncle had gotten him a job as a grocery stockboy after he'd finished art school and shown no inclination of applying for jobs in that field—and then headed home after, all in a daze, handling his assigned chores well enough but too distracted to do much more than grunt when people spoke to him.

He had magic. There was no other word for it. Something had changed, in him, in the world, in the stars, but whatever it was, his art was suddenly filled with magic. He could bring images to life, if only for a moment.

But, really, what could he do with that?

He couldn't draw money—it would fade before he could spend it. And besides, what did he care about money? His needs were few, since he still lived with his aunt and uncle, as he had since his parents had died. His job provided enough for him to contribute and have pocket money for going out with friends. What else mattered?

So, what use was this strange new gift, really? His illusion pieces would be that much more convincing—truly real—for a few seconds. Big deal. In a way, that was actually worse. It was one thing when someone tripped over the pothole he'd drawn, cursing as they realized they'd fallen for it. But what if someone actually fell in and hurt themselves? Which, he now realized with a shock, had been a danger all along, but was even more so now. And the idea that his art could have actually hurt someone? Not cool. Not funny.

No, this new skill was a neat trick, and nice that it maybe connected him more with his mother. But that was all.

Art resolved not to use it, or think about it, any further. It didn't matter.

—

"Shameful," his uncle remarked that night, folding the newspaper and setting it aside as Auntie Jayatri brought out dinner. Chandran was old-fashioned enough to still buy print papers. "Did you see?" He stabbed a finger down at an image on the page. "Disgraceful."

"What is, dear?" Jayatri asked, setting down a bowl of steaming basmati rice alongside one holding lamb curry. She squeezed his shoulder fondly in passing, and Chandran reached up to cup her hand in return, but his scowl did not abate.

"This museum," he explained. "The Chandler. A limited showing of 'culturally significant items.' Including this!"

Art scooted his seat around so he could crane his neck and study the image. It showed a beautifully intricate brass lamp with three tiers, each containing several small, shallow bowls to cup oil and flame. "An Adukku Vilakku?" The tiered Deeparadhana lamps were used in evening rituals at Hindu temples, their flames presented to images of the deities to denote respect. Still, he didn't see what had his uncle so worked up. "But you can buy those online," he pointed out.

"Not this one, you cannot," Chandran retorted, his face red. "This is from Mundeshwari itself."

Jayatri gasped, and even Art startled a bit at the statement. The Mundeshwari temple in Bihar was thought to be one of the oldest

Hindu temples in the world. He'd read recently that the building had been conclusively dated back to 108 CE! "But isn't that a protected site?" he asked. They'd done a section on temple art in school, and had learned about conservation and protection.

"It is," his uncle agreed. As a member of the Historic Preservation Society, he would know about such things. "But that does not mean some pieces have not found their way into private collections. Proving they were misappropriated and then reclaiming them?" He shook his head. "It is a long and difficult process, and these people often have deep pockets. And now one of those thieves has the audacity to openly display it? Terrible!"

It was. For once, Art found himself in complete agreement with his uncle. That lamp belonged back at the temple, not in some rich man's private museum! He knew Chandran was right, though. It could take years for the authorities to agree that the artifact had to be returned. And then, like as not, the owner would "misplace" it—and it would never go back home.

Not unless someone did something about it. Something more direct.

—

That weekend, Art took himself to the Chandler. He'd been once before, on a school trip. It was a handsome building, to be sure—all granite blocks, clean and square and large enough to be imposing, with tall, thin windows cut deep into the heavy walls. Inside were marble floors and high, vaulted ceilings and towering, paneled metal doors. The lighting was subdued, and the exhibits were in darkened rooms with spotlights over each glass case, like tiny islands of light in a dark sea. Visitors were vague shadows, swimming from one item to the next.

He made a full circuit of the room, studying each exhibit in turn before stopping at the lamp. No more than two feet high, its burnished surface showed its age in the patina of the metal and the light pitting time had wrought on its once smooth surface. Enough other people circulated about that Art didn't linger there, but he made note of the display's location, and of the room's general layout—as well as marking the security cameras tucked away discreetly in the corners, up where wall met ceiling. Good to know his time spent sneaking his art into public spaces was good for something!

Getting in and out of the building itself would be an issue, as would avoiding the guards he'd seen strolling throughout, studying each and every attendee. Then there was the problem of the display itself.

Art had a great deal to think about. He did not feel overwhelmed, however. Instead, he found the challenge energizing, his mind and spirit aligned. This was the right thing to do. And he was beginning to have an idea of how to manage, as well.

For once, his art would mean something, do something, serve something.

He hoped Uncle Chandran would be proud.

———

The next day, Art returned. He was wearing a loose-fitting hoodie, a messenger bag slung over his shoulder. The guards inspected the bag as he entered, and found only his sketchpad and pencils with three canvas rolls tucked beneath. "School assignment," he explained with a shrug, and got noncommittal grunts in return. Museums were used to art students sketching their exhibits.

Once inside, Art wandered a few of the permanent installations before choosing a spot in the main hall across from an oil portrait. There, he stationed himself against the wall, sketchbook in hand, and waited for his chance. Guards in places like this followed a strict schedule, including a shift change. That would be his moment.

Sure enough, a short while later he saw the guard heading for the front and its security desk. Another had appeared from a side door and was already waiting to make the handoff and take over patrol.

That was when Art pulled the fire alarm right by his head, covering the motion by leaning forward and angling his pad as if to get a better view of the painting across the way.

Sirens began blaring instantly, and lights flashed from the boxes placed all along the hall and in each room. All the guards sprang into action, the two already standing rushing to shepherd people out while the one at the desk made announcements urging everyone to leave in an orderly fashion.

No one noticed Art ducking into the bathroom just behind him.

It was a cold space, all white and black marble. Art went straight to the middle stall, knelt in front of it, and pulled out one of the canvas rolls. He laid that flat and began sketching. He knew he'd only have a minute.

The work done, he slipped into the stall, hopping up to perch on the toilet. The canvas he held up and fastened to the sides with small alligator clips he'd pulled from the bag's front pouch.

He'd only just gotten the image in place when he heard the bathroom door open. "Anyone in here?" a voice called out. "Fire alarm, I need everyone out." Then came the sound of the first stall being opened. Then the second.

And then the third, the one Art was in.

The door banged open, slammed against the side, and swung shut again. Even before it had bounced all the way back, the next two stalls had been checked and then footsteps and the sound of the main door indicated the guard leaving again. Having seen nothing but five empty stalls.

Whew.

Unclipping his picture of an empty stall, Art rolled that back up and returned it to his bag, pulling the second roll out in its place and exiting the stall to draw a quick but unfinished sketch on that surface.

Then he slipped out of the bathroom, checking before he opened the door by the simple expedient of drawing a spyhole on its blank metal face. Confirming that the coast was clear, he eased out into the hall and hurried into the special exhibit, where he paused just long enough to add the last stroke to the current sketch before walking quickly to the lamp, holding the canvas in front of him.

All anyone watching the monitors would see was unbroken shadow and an empty room, the image he'd created blending into the rest of the space.

Reaching the glass case, Art moved to its rear and took out a grease pencil. He drew a quick panel across most of the pane there, complete with hinges and a simple closure. Unlatching that, he swung the panel open, reached in, and grabbed the lamp, which he quickly pulled out and stuck into his bag before shutting the panel. He'd barely closed it again before the hinges and latch smeared, leaving an unbroken glass pane with some dark smudges along its side, though he couldn't resist adding a few additional marks to those before turning away.

Hiding behind his canvas shroud, Art hurried from the room. There were still visitors being ushered out, the process slowed by the guards checking each bag, and he fell into line with the rest, extracting the last canvas as he did. This one was far smaller than the other two, and the sketch he applied was of his messenger bag itself, specifically the interior lining. He finished that and draped it over the lamp just as he was reaching the front of the line, handing the whole bag off to the guard there.

The man opened it, saw only the sketchpad and pencils, and handed it back, waving Art through.

He didn't breathe properly until he was out on the sidewalk, bag over his shoulder, lamp safely nestled within. Then it was all Art could do not to whoop and cheer. He'd done it!

"Uncle?" Art tapped on the door.

Chandran glanced up, surprised. "Arvind? Is everything all right?" Which was a fair question, since Art hadn't visited his uncle's workplace in many years. It was still as clean and organized as ever, though.

"It is." Art stepped in, shutting the door behind him. "It's just—I needed to give you this. I hoped you could get it back to its home." And, reaching into his bag, he withdrew the lamp and set it on the desk, the polished brass gleaming in the harsh overhead light.

"What?" Chandran sat up, staring at the object before lifting it with shaking hands. "The Adukku Vilakku from Mundeshwari? How?"

Art shrugged, trying to suppress his grin. "It didn't belong there, in that place."

"No, it did not." When his uncle looked up at him, there was something in his eyes Art had not seen in a long time. Pride. "I will see it restored to the Mundeshwari right away," he promised, rising to his feet. "'Recovered by an anonymous benefactor,' we will say." He set a hand on Art's shoulder, then pulled him into a quick hug. "I do not know how you accomplished this, Arvind, but it is good," he said, his words muted by the contact. "You have done a good thing."

Art returned the hug, then stepped back, brushing the tears from his eyes. "Thank you, uncle," was all he trusted himself to say as he let himself back out. But inside he was singing. This was the path his auntie had spoken of, that his uncle had dreamed of and urged for. This was what he could do with his talent.

He wondered what the owners of the Chandler would think when they discovered the lamp missing? Or when they found his note? He had left only two words, but they'd seemed fitting, and he thought his uncle might have even been amused if he'd read them:

"Art out."

Aaron Rosenberg is the author of the best-selling *DuckBob* SF comedy series, the Relicant Chronicles epic fantasy series, the *Dread Remora* space-opera series, and, with David Niall Wilson, the *O.C.L.T.* occult thriller series. His tie-in work contains novels for *Star Trek, Warhammer, World of WarCraft, Stargate: Atlantis, Shadowrun,* and *Eureka* and short stories for *The X-Files, World of Darkness, Crusader Kings II, Master of Orion,* and *Europa Universalis IV.* He has written children's books (including the award-winning *Bandslam: The Junior Novel* and the #1 best-selling *42: The Jackie Robinson Story*), educational books, and roleplaying games (including the Origins Award-winning *Gamemastering Secrets*). Aaron lives in New York. You can follow him online at gryphonrose.com, at facebook.com/gryphonrose, and on Twitter @gryphonrose.

Shattered

Marie Bilodeau

THE FIRST PIECE I found in a blooming rosebush.

The second within a stone circle.

The third, on the edge of a volcano.

And so many others. By a babbling brook. In the heart of a peach. On the sole of a shoe. In the cracks of an old staircase.

For years, I gathered them.

Years, turning to decades.

And still, I cannot find my way back to you.

—

You look at me, smiling. New dress sparkling with moonlight corralled from the sky. Stars dance around your necklace, created from carefully harvested hopes. Feet finely draped with the caress of gentle night songs, to help us dance the darkness away.

I hold out my hand.

Finely covered in silver rings, dangling bracelets. My dress created of the wilds of the earth. Of vines and buds just daring to bloom. Of the scent of roses dipped in summer's heat.

You take it, laugh.

I don't know what happened. Why did the mirror, who'd guided me to you, suddenly shatter?

—

I thought I'd found the last piece by the crumbling castle.

So little was still missing. Such a small piece, a hole in its center.

But I needed it whole, so I could ask the mirror: *Why did you take her from me?*

And how do I find her again?

———

You weren't a reflection. But you started as a dream.

You didn't step out of the mirror. But it showed me the way to you.

Through moonlit meadows and fears. Through briars and thorns.

Scratched, torn and bleeding, I found you.

Or was it that you, from your glass perch in the sky, found me?

———

The piece from the castle fits perfectly.

But one shard is missing, still.

One tiny sliver, and the mirror stays silent, ignoring my cries. My screams. My pleas.

Just for one glimpse of you, I promise my very soul.

And yet, it does not answer.

———

"The darkness will keep us safe," I insist, wild and afraid. An animal seeking the safety of burrows.

"The light will set us free," you reply, soothing.

And we find the castle, and the ball.

And we dance, and dance, until all eyes are on us.

Until the mirror shatters.

I kneel by the mirror, my dress in tatters, years marked on my features, unkind.

How do I go on, knowing our story will only end in tears? Knowing there is no happily ever after for us?

How do I keep seeking you, seeking the light, when darkness has spread everywhere in your absence?

How do I keep believing I can fix something when I still cannot fathom why it broke?

"Amelia," you say, whisps of light dancing around every syllable. I love when you say my name. A simple word turned to a caress.

"Beloved," I answer. Always. For you hate your name, which they'd hurt you with, jeered at you with, turned it to cruel nicknames as they abandoned you in ashes.

And you smile, because of how I'd said it. And you lean into me.

As I lean into you.

"Why," I whisper, as broken as the mirror, as hollow as the reflection, as dull as its surface. "Was this not the story you wanted me to tell? Not the ending your craved?"

Selfish. The mirror had been selfish. To show me the light. To give me hope. And then to take it. Or to let it vanish.

Why had the mirror shattered, just when I'd finally felt whole?

You hold out your hand, pulling me toward that light. Always toward the light.

But I want to hold back. To stay in the shadows. In my burrow, comfortable, warm, familiar.

Where the mirror awaits. Where it had kept me company, for so long, showing me the world outside. Thinking I would never leave it.

Until it showed me you. Believing that your light would scare me.

But how it didn't. How it called me to you. How it calls me to you, still, even though I dwell in darkness, awaiting your return.

———

The darkness was safe, Beloved. It's the light that shattered the mirror. It's the light that took you from me.

I curl up in the darkness, by the mirror with its missing shard.

———

"You've eaten too much poison," you argue.

"I've known the apples' roots for a long time," I reply. "I helped them grow."

"Not everything that stems from us is good," you whisper.

You, whose beauty created a constellation, shattered glass slippers forming stars you rode to escape your would-be captors.

Every light creates a shadow. The brighter the light, the deeper the shadow.

And you, Beloved, cast a deep shadow. And it is in its darkness that I now dwell.

———

I stand, heart weary, but feet stepping into a slow dance. Under the moonlight, so pale without your glow.

I close my eyes, imagine you in my arms.

"They stare because of your beauty," you'd say, breathless as we danced.

"No, because of yours," I'd say, blushing.

"Or," a crooked smile on your lips, "because we know the steps much better than they do!"

And we'd laughed.

And the mirror shattered.

———

I gaze at the mirror, its surface reflecting only a sliver of light. The only light I'd known as a child.

But a dark light, keeping me trapped here, promising joy and only providing captivity.

And I understand.

The laughter, Beloved. The laughter broke it. Joy like a wave over it, a ripple it could not stand.

Would not take.

No. Not your laughter. *Mine,* which joined yours, teased out of me by your effervescence.

My laughter was more than it could bear, for it signalled my acceptance of the light.

———

"I won't come back," I whisper, my own reflection dull. "The final piece will always be missing, won't it? No matter what I do. How far I look. I'll never find it, because you don't want me to."

A deep breath. Earth, roots, life.

"I won't come back." I turn to go.

I almost make it out, until it calls me back, lures me to it, as it always did before you came, Beloved. The missing shard in the slight light of the mirror fails to reflect only one part of my body.

My heart missing from my own reflection.

—

"It's your heart I love best," you whisper, naked skin flushed.

"My heart is earth and roots," I grimace. "Old and worn, and hidden in darkness."

You laugh. That laughter I didn't yet know how to join. Roll atop me. Kiss me fiercely, tasting of stardust and hope.

"Amelia," you say, eyes holding mine captive, "that's what I need to stay grounded. I need your heart, and nothing else."

—

My heart is missing in the reflection.

A heart beat. And another.

And I understand where the missing shard is. Where you hid it, mirror. Where you thought I'd never look again. Where I'd never dare see it.

In my heart.

You hid the final shard in my heart, even as you ripped my Beloved from me.

—

I stumble from the burrow, desperate for light, heart thudding in my chest.

I can feel the sliver, now. Edges against strong muscle that weathered storm, withstood floods and fires, helped lift up villages and lives.

I feel it, and I cannot ignore it. For years, I've waited for you, Beloved.

For centuries.

Beneath my feet, I feel the power of the mirror. Calling me back. To darkness. To safety.

But it's to the sky that I look as I reach for the shard within my heart.

It's to you, Beloved, that I look. To you, and your strength that shattered a glass slipper and turned it to stardust. To find freedom. To break free of the tyranny of expectations. Of a kingdom.

Of a story.

I want to be free, too! Away from the mirror. Away from the darkness. Away from the world that promised all but only took and took, leaving me raw.

Shattered.

I look to you, Beloved, as I find the last shard and pry it out, as it cuts artery and organ, lets loose my life blood. As it vanishes back into the now complete mirror.

As I crumple to the ground, looking up. Up toward the light.

Toward you.

———

Blinking slowly, I hear it, in the distant sky. Your laughter. Cascading down, set free as easily as my breath.

Starlight dances in your hair. Your eyes are made of silver.

"I freed you," I whisper. Or perhaps just think it.

"You freed your beautiful heart, and brought me back to you." You gather me in your arms, lift me up, take me away from the darkness. I smile, your warmth coating me, the beats of my heart growing as strong as yours.

And I lean into you. As you lean into me.

Beloved.

⸻

Marie Bilodeau is a French Canadian author and storyteller who writes mostly in English because, as her family would say, she's contrary. Her speculative fiction has won several awards and been translated into Chinese and French (to her family's delight, though they still believe her to be contrary). Marie is also a storyteller and has told stories (in both languages!) across Canada in theatres, tea shops, at festivals and under disco balls. Find out more at mariebilodeau.com.

Flower Girl

Donald J. Bingle

OLENA SAT ON THE STOOP in the alleyway soaking up the bright rays of the sun on her cool skin. Normally, she would be doing chores at this time of day—folding laundry as her mother pulled it from the retractable line that could stretch across the broken concrete of the narrow space between apartment buildings or fetching a missing ingredient from the corner shop needed for cooking supper later. But today was not a normal day. None of the days were normal anymore, of course, not since the fighting began, but today was special. Not better, most likely, but special all the same. Today was her seventh birthday.

She turned her head to one side so the light would warm the previously shaded part of her face and caught the soft sound of the apartment door opening. She listened closer and heard heavy boots lightly treading inside.

"Did you find something?" her mother whispered. "Anything? I can go out and look if you had no luck."

"Just this," came the reply in the hoarse, soft breath of her father. "It . . . it's not much, but choices were few and the prices beyond reach for most. And I had little time to search." His voice became firmer and sadder. "I have to report."

Olena heard a gentle rustle of paper unfolding and a sharp intake of breath from her mother as her father continued on. "I wanted to find a doll or a new dress or . . ."

"No, no," protested her mother. "This is better. This will do fine."

Olena heard her mother step toward the door, as if to call for her, but her father interrupted.

"Don't call her in yet," he said, his voice low, but not at all gruff. "We should say our goodbyes first."

"How long will you be gone?"

"A week, a month. Perhaps a year. But, with how things are going . . ." Her father's low voice cracked. "Most likely a lifetime."

She heard a few sniffles and murmurs from her mother, but could not make out the words.

"Sometimes," her father replied, "I think of how vibrant and green and fresh everything was on the evening we first met in the forest."

"You mean when we danced in the circle of flowers and I first ensnared you with . . ." She heard her mother giggle. ". . . my *charms*."

"I was stunned when I first met you. More beautiful than any flower, your eyes twinkling in the gloaming." He chuckled. "I was more enraptured than captured. A more-than-willing companion the entire time. I was even more stunned when the dance and my holiday ended and you agreed to come back to the city with me, far from all you knew."

"Your mother and your brother's widow, they both needed you here." She sighed. "Though, sometimes I wish we were back in the forest."

"We made our own magic right here. *Olena*." He let out a deep breath. "This place is our home. She has never known anyplace, but here. And, I will do my best to protect our home and our homeland from the invaders. Duty still calls and honor answers the call." His voice grew louder. "Call her in. I have to go soon."

Once again, her mother stepped toward the door. "Olena! Come see what your father brought you."

Olena stood and turned, waited a few moments, then opened the back door into the kitchen, taking a deep breath and exhaling just as she bustled in, so her mother would think she'd just run from down the alley, rather than listening from the stoop.

The first thing she noticed was that her father was in his full combat gear and that his pack and weapon were leaning against the wall near the front door. The second was that both her parents were looking directly at her and smiling. Tears welled from their eyes, and their smiles were sad, even weary, but still genuine. The third was a small rectangular package wrapped in brown paper, neatly folded at either end. Her mother held it out to her.

"Your father got this special for you."

Olena took the package and shook it. Nothing rattled. Not too heavy, but very uniform in the distribution of the weight. She had no idea what it could be.

"Well, go ahead," urged her father. "Open it."

She unfolded the crinkled flap at one end, like she knew her mother must have, just moments before, and peered in, angling the mysterious gift so light would shine in enough to see and read the biggest word on the side of the cardboard box inside.

"Chalk?" she said.

"Not just chalk," her mother said. "Colored chalk."

"You can use it to play hopscotch in the alley," her father suggested.

"Oh," she replied as she finished unwrapping the dusty, thin cardboard box. The box looked big enough to hold more chalk than even the teachers had at school. More than she could ever use for hopscotch.

"See?" Her mother pointed at the smaller text on the carton. "Along with regular, white chalk, there's more than two dozen different shades—an entire bouquet of colors. It's special chalk. The kind artists use to draw." Olena saw a twinkle in her mother's eyes as she continued. "It's magic and wonderful, just like you."

Only a few minutes later, her father was gone and tears streaked down her mother's cheeks as the two of them were left on their own. After a bit, her mother took the box of chalk and handed it to her.

"You should go play and have fun."

Olena shrugged. "There's no one to play hopscotch with but old man Karpenko, and he's always so grouchy, I don't think he even knows what fun is." She scrunched up her nose at the thought of their sour neighbor. "Probably couldn't hop that well anyway," she added. "He uses a cane because of his limp."

"It's true, I've never seen him smile or heard him call out a happy greeting. But, did you ever think he might be unhappy, even unpleasant, for the same reason he limps? Maybe his foot hurts all the time." Her mother's face lightened and she nodded toward the door. "You don't need a playmate, anyway. It's a beautiful, sunny day. You should always grab beauty when you can." She tapped the box. "Draw some pictures while the concrete is still dry. They say it will snow later."

At first, Olena didn't know what to draw. She started with a plain white hopscotch grid and played solo a few times, but that wasn't really that much fun. So she dug into the colors and started decorating her stoop with flowers and grass, along with drawings of bunnies hiding in the greenery. Her designs grew bolder and larger, extending from the stoop and down the alley. She was adding a bumblebee to one of the flowers—delicate lines were difficult to do with the thick, blunt edges of the fat fingers of chalk—when old man Karpenko scared her with a sudden shout.

"What foolishness is this? You're vandalizing my property."

So much for her hopes he would just stay inside today. "I'm just drawing pictures on the alley. I haven't touched your apartment building. And the colors are pretty."

"The side of the alley next to my apartment *is* my property," scowled the old man. "Besides, bright colors like that can draw attention ..." He pointed his cane toward the sky, where gray clouds had begun to roll in and block the sun. "... from anyone watching from up there."

Olena screwed up her face. "You mean, from the apartments above ours?"

"No, silly girl. From the sky! These days, you don't want to draw any attention from the sky." He leaned on his cane and reached down, snatching up the piece of white chalk from next to her box and limping over to the back door to his apartment. He scrawled a large symbol comprised of angled lines on the door, then tossed the chalk back toward the box.

Olena had never liked the man, but he was even scarier and nastier than she'd ever seen him before. And what he'd drawn made no sense to her. She knew her numbers and letters and this wasn't one. She pointed at his door. "What's that stand for? What's it mean?"

Karpenko snorted. "It doesn't stand for anything, anything at all, but it *means* that I might not be killed when the men watching from above get here." He opened the door to his kitchen, set down his cane and grabbed a broom, then started sweeping his side of the alley. His broad, clumsy strokes smeared the chalk, destroying most of her hopscotch grid and several of her nicer flower drawings. He leaned on his broom after only a few minutes and looked up to the sky. "Bah. The snow will get the rest soon enough," he said as he limped back inside.

Now that there were clouds blocking the sun, it was much colder, but Olena wasn't about to let a mean old man spoil her birthday or her art, so she kept drawing. She kept to her side of the alley, leaving the home rectangle from her ruined hopscotch in place, but expanding around it and down the alley. She abandoned the smaller, more detailed type of art she had started with, instead filling space with large, colorful flowers. Not just red, yellow, green, purple, blue, and orange, but teal and pink and more. The larger and brighter the better.

Finally, she retreated to her home rectangle and looked at her handiwork, spreading out before her down the alley. She was proud of what she'd done and delighted with her present. As the light grew dimmer, she half-closed her eyes and imagined it extending farther, beyond the end of the alley and out in all directions—a place of color and beauty and magic and happiness. She held out her chalk-dusted hands in front of her, reveling in the colors arrayed on them, sparkling in the bright sunshine, dusting away in puffs in the warm breeze . . .

She blinked. Sunshine? Warm breeze?

She opened her eyes wide and looked about. She was standing in a gently sloping meadow, with gaily-colored flowers all about her and woods in the near distance. Birds chirped. Bees buzzed. Garden flowers of every variety—and some she'd never seen or imagined—wafted in the breeze, scenting the air with a thousand sweet and pleasing aromas.

She wheeled about. No alley, no buildings, no cement, no clouds, nobody watching from above, and no nasty old neighbors. Here, there was only joy and magic; nothing to fear at all. She started to run toward the woods, but then heard something behind her and turned to look back. In the distance she saw a gray portal hovering atop the path, the crisp edges forming a rectangle the size of her hopscotch home. And she heard a faraway voice in the distance from that same spot, calling her name.

"Olena! Olena!"

Her mother was calling for her.

The field of flowers and the woods ahead beckoned her, too, but she could not ignore her mother's voice. She started back toward the gray rectangle at a slow, trudging pace. But then she noticed that the gray rectangle was blurring at the edges and slowly turning white and shimmering. As it did, it grew smaller and smaller. Was it closing?

She ran.

She ran faster than she'd ever run at school or play. She ran for her life.

Just as it seemed as if the rectangle would disappear, Olena found herself at her back stoop just as her mother opened the door.

"Oh, there you are. I'd given up calling back here and tried calling out the front door." She looked past Olena to the alleyway and frowned. "I'm sorry, I didn't get a good look at your drawings before the snow covered them up. It must have started while I was soaking laundry. Did you have fun?"

Olena nodded dully and looked over her shoulder to the alleyway. Snow covered everything. No chalk could be seen, except for the box on the stoop and a large white symbol on Karpenko's grimy door.

As she grabbed up her present, her magical chalk, she noticed there were no tracks in the snow. No tracks at all.

Weeks passed. Cold and snow and rain trapped them inside. That and the sounds of distant explosions and gunfire from near the river. Mother tried to keep it from her, but Olena was smart enough to know that things were getting worse in the world, especially *her* world. She saw strange men in the street with weapons, lumbering vehicles with large gun barrels, and columns of smoke from the direction of the commercial district. The explosions and gunfire crept closer every day. Her mother stopped going to market and their portions of food got smaller and smaller with each meal.

One dark night a man came to the door and spoke with her mother in hushed tones. Her mother pressed a handkerchief to her face to cover the noise of her sudden crying out, then stumbled back to bed. Olena heard her sobbing all night. She asked the next day if anything was wrong, but her mother denied that anything bad had happened. She kept saying everything would be fine, but Olena knew better. She was very sure something very bad *had* happened. Olena knew what that must be even as she refused to believe it could possibly be true. But, despite the deep, dark emptiness she felt deep inside, she did her best to be, or at least pretend to be, brave like her mother.

Still, spring was coming and not even bad men and the pain of unimaginable loss could stop the world from spinning into a new season. Birds chirped and plants—mostly weeds—sprang forth from the ground. Olena kept careful track of the days, for she knew her parents' anniversary was fast approaching and she wanted to do something wonderful and magical as a present for her, to brighten up what would be a sad day filled with only the hollow echoes of better times.

A bright, warm ray of sunshine woke her when the day arrived.

She dressed quickly and grabbed her box of colored chalk, sneaking out even before her mother got up to make their meager breakfast. Using a folded kitchen towel as a cushion, she knelt on the concrete and started her special project.

She began with a large rectangle marked home, then spread out from there with the brightest, most vivid flowers she could envision. Poppies and roses and tulips and lilies and more. Wild flowers and imaginary flowers and lush green grasses. She drew and drew and drew, colors mingling, dust covering her hands and clothes, but she refused to slow or stop until the entire alley—both sides—was filled with color and joy. And on the doorway to their kitchen she drew tall, bright sunflowers against a cobalt blue sky.

And when everything was ready, she stood on the home rectangle and half-closed her eyes until her magic world once more appeared, with more and brighter flowers in the field surrounding her and a path to the woods straight ahead. Then, Olena turned and went back through the home rectangle and into the kitchen. She would take her mother on a magical holiday to her wondrous world of color and delight. You had to grab beauty every chance you could get, after all.

Her mother cried out in joy when she saw what Olena had done, but Olena insisted there was still more. She took her mother's hand and pulled her to the home rectangle.

"Hold my hand," Olena said. "And, half-close your eyes."

Mother and child stood in the alley, silent and still, as the dirty, burning city disappeared from view and a magical world of color and warmth and peace shimmered into existence. And this time, when her mother wept, Olena knew it was tears of joy.

Suddenly, the peace and happiness of the moment was shattered by a rumbling explosion and a shrill and angry voice. "Here. Over here!"

Olena knew what was happening. Old man Karpenko had betrayed them to the bad men with guns.

She ran.

She ran faster than she'd ever run at school or play. She ran for her life.

But this time, she ran away from the home rectangle. She ran for the safety of the woods.

And, when she dared to look back over her shoulder, she saw that the home rectangle had gone from gray to bright red and was shimmering and blurring at the edges.

Blood. It had to be blood, sealing the entrance . . . and exit . . . to the magical world her art, her magic . . . and her mother's magic . . . had created in a cruel, dark world.

Olena cried out and stumbled, almost falling from the thought her mother had sacrificed herself for her deliverance from evil.

But that was also when Olena realized her mother was still holding her hand, running with her toward the mystery and the magic of the forest. There was beauty and wonder and safety in the forest where her mother had once danced gaily with her father, but chose to follow him into the city, where her magic was limited, but her love unbounded.

Olena suddenly understood what the strange angled symbol stood for. It stood for death. And, old man Karpenko had reaped what he had sown.

But, Olena had sown flowers and joy. Now she and her mother would reap a bountiful harvest of happiness and peace.

Donald J. Bingle was the world's top-ranked player of classic RPGA roleplaying tournaments for the last fifteen years of the last century, but has more recently shifted his creative endeavors to writing fiction. He has authored eight books and more than sixty shorter stories in the fantasy, science fiction, horror, thriller, mystery, steampunk, comedy, and memoir genres. His books include the Dick Thornby Spy Thriller Series and, with Jean Rabe, The Love-Haight Case Files, an award-winning urban fantasy series about lawyers defending the legal rights of supernatural creatures in a magic-filled San Francisco. Here's what Says Ed Greenwood, creator of The Forgotten Realms, had to say about Don's first novel, *Forced Conversion:* "I loved it! Many writers have explored hard-hitting and brutal possible futures for Earth, and told colorful tales of people trying to stay alive in them, but few have brought such imagined futures as vividly to life as Don Bingle—and no other book I can think of examines how and why such a future might just happen as well as FORCED CONVERSION does—or provides half the breath-catching twists and turns of Bingle's yarn . . . Highly recommended!" More on Don and his writing at donaldjbingle.com.

A Genrenauts story

Michael R. Underwood

MALLERY YORK was born for Broadway.

But Broadway wasn't getting the memo.

The heat of summer filled the air with the scents of sewage, sweat, and stress as Mallery strode through uneven crowds. There were just enough tourists mixed in to stymie the speed-walking New Yorkers. She'd become one quickly, crossing avenues to race between auditions and two jobs to make rent on a room the size of a bathroom. A child's bathroom.

She was twenty minutes late getting out of work due to a call-out from another server and a surprise rush with a German tourist group. At least she got to practice her pronunciation.

No time to touch up her makeup, no time to warm up on the subway instead of hoofing it.

Mallery entered the hallway, revealing a dozen gorgeous women in stunning makeup. Perfect curls, dagger-sharp cat-eyes, and show-stopper lipstick in every shade. After the first time she lost a role to an ex, she promised herself she would never try to pick up women at auditions again.

But there were few things more intoxicating than the combination of talent and ambition.

She managed to fix her hair and reapply her gloss in the hallway mirror, but a harried-looking intern called her in before she could warm up.

Mallery stood, dropped her shoulders back, and put on her game face.

She'd spent three years making a serious go at the Broadway life, and while she worked steadily, it was always Off-Broadway, at the edges of the scene but never making the main stage.

This audition barely qualified – ensemble for a *Mamma Mia* revival, but each role led to another, and at least this one played to her strengths in comedy.

The casting table sat three. Three? There was the director Georgi French, fresh off a Grammy for the live TV production of *My Fair Lady*, with his trademark black turtleneck and big circular glasses; producer Karoline Versa in a structured three-piece suit and pink hair in a pompadour, and . . . who was this? Forty-something, Black, broad-shouldered, short hair, with searching eyes.

She wracked her brain trying to match a face to a name, but as she hit her spot she gave up.

"Mallery York," the intern said, and the three pulled out her headshot/resume sheet.

She handed her sheet music to the pianist and returned to her spot.

"Broadway Baby" was a risky choice for an audition song, almost too on-the-nose. Mallery had decided to lean into it, channeling her nervous energy into making the song into a self-effacing comedic piece. She couldn't stand out just trying to be Bernadette Peters or any of the performers who had brought the song to life before. She had to make the song her own.

The seated trio kept their poker faces up, giving her nothing. That was the worst part about auditions. In a real show, you had a whole room to work with. The circuit was closed, energy moving back and forth, giving you something to react to and send. Instead, Georgi, Karoline, and the mysterious third figure communicated in tiny gestures and glances, but they were indecipherable for Mallery, so she blocked them out to focus on her performance.

At least the pianist was having fun, embellishing and playing with relish. Probably glad to not be playing from the list of the same handful of songs that were popular for women's auditions at any given time.

Georgi French raised a hand just two verses in, cutting her off. She'd had worse at auditions, but she'd had better.

"Thank you," Karoline added.

The intern started moving, and that was it. Mallery gave a short curtsy and left, holding in her frustration and disappointment.

Never let them see you crack. A bad audition could cost you a role, but expressing frustration or defeat, well, that was somehow an unconscionable display of unprofessionalism despite being a human being who was trying to get a job because of their ability to convey emotion, not because they were a singing dancing robot.

Mallery checked her phone walking out past the hallway of rival-colleagues. Two hours until dance class, then a blissful evening without working her second job at the sports bar.

Out of habit, she checked her professional email address coming out of the dance class. She had a message, but not from Georgi or an assistant.

Who is Angstrom King?

"I had the fortune of sitting in on your audition today and hoped you'd be available on very short notice to participate in a run-through. I've had a last-second cancellation and could use your talents. I've enclosed my credentials."

Mallery hadn't heard pf him, but he'd produced three off-Broadway shows and was an associate professor of Comparative Literature at the University of Maryland. Then he quoted a *very* generous retainer for three hours of work. Like, her food & utilities for the month generous.

This was weird, even for Broadway, but she was three months into juggling credit cards and close to going absolutely broke and having to move home. So she texted a friend the location where she was going, switched into the work shoes she could run in, and made sure the pepper spray was still in her purse.

Which is how Mallery found herself in the Meatpacking district in a warehouse she'd sworn had already been converted into condos. But instead of a lobby or a freight elevator, she walked into another reception room. The mysterious third person stood as she entered.

"Good. I wasn't sure you'd be available. I'm Angstrom King." King wore the same suit as before, but had a warmer manner, poker face gone.

"Nice to meet you. What's the script?"

"It's an experimental immersive experience." He opened a set of double doors, revealing a mostly-empty warehouse with a massive pile of boxes or something under a tarp and a loft apartment up in a corner.

Oh, he's one of those *weirdos,* Mallery thought. Some rich eccentric, maybe a family friend of some bigtime producer. Weird format, strange location, the generous paycheck. As long as the money was good.

"So where's the rest of the cast?" She glanced around, hand fishing around in her purse for the pepper spray just in case.

"The run-through isn't here." King tapped his phone, and the stack of whatever under the tarp vanished, revealing a no-shit, thirty-foot-tall Buck Rogers spaceship.

"You built a spaceship for your set? Does it open up? What was that hologram thing? How do you fit an audience in there?" She repeated the paycheck to herself, hoping that if she indulged King's oddities, he'd reveal his real plan early enough for her to be safe.

"The run-through isn't there, either. The spaceship is real."

Mallery started walking backward, fear spiking. "Is this a kidnapping? A bizarrely elaborate mega-rich kidnapping to murder me on some private island?"

"No, it's a dimension-jumping spaceship and I'm offering you an audition for the best role of your life."

Bleeding-edge holograms and a personal spaceship. That plus a high four-figure check for a read-through made three impossible things in one day. The smart thing to do would be to turn around and leave. Find another way to make money, pretend none of this ever happened.

But even if this guy wasn't on the level, Mallery had dreamed of being an astronaut as a little girl, and she could still make a break for it after taking a look around in his very expensive prop . . .

———

King talked his way through a several-minute launch process, out of habit and rigor or for her benefit, maybe both. She tugged at the straps of her harness and spun her rings, at least hoping this thing would shine some pretty lights.

In times like this, what Mallery wanted to do was talk. But it was a bad idea to distract your pilot in normal situations, and she imagined that somehow traveling between dimensions was no different? Assuming this wasn't all a prank show or the convoluted kidnapping M.O. of some truly ludicrous billionaire.

But all doubts vanished when the thrust kicked in, slamming her against the seat as the view of the warehouse ceiling was replaced with coruscating lights out of a prestige science fiction TV show.

"What the?!" she gasped as King guided the ship through gentle banks and dives. "This is real? How do you know which way is what?"

King gave a gentle smile. "We have very good navigation technology and the best staff money can afford."

"Whose money?" Mallery had learned to find out as much as possible about who held the purse-strings after a show collapsed because the financiers turned out to be middle-men for a particularly incompetent VC techbro.

"The founders made a lot of money the first few years after discovering this technology, mostly stealing from assorted villains and reclaiming precious materials from post-apocalyptic worlds without anyone in a position to use them."

"Huh. That's." Mallery tried wrapping her brain around the implications. It reminded her of some novel she'd read a decade prior, though that one had a fantasy vibe. If he had a real rocket ship or good enough effects to mimic one, the holographic technology, then this was either real or her desperation to not give up on Broadway was landing her in one of the most preposterous ways to die.

"Hold on, we're landing." The technicolor starscape was replaced by another warehouse ceiling. A very familiar ceiling.

"Wait. Is this the same building?"

"Close enough. The organization owns a lot of warehouses as hangars and safehouses."

The thrust vanished as the ship settled in. Except none of the physics made sense.

"I understand that this is all very strange, but I promise we're not trying to trick you or hurt you. Follow me out. The rest of my team is here, they'll brief you on the situation."

In for a penny, in for a pound, Mallery thought, poking her head out of the ship at a nearly-identical warehouse. But this one was occupied. A tall, muscular person with light tanned skin stood by a table covered in disassembled guns. To his left, a curvy older person with brown skin sat in front of a trio of monitors, wearing a sandy brown duster.

"Hi!" Mallery said, waving out the window. When in doubt, charm offensive.

The older of the two stood from the computers and walked over to offer a hand and a "Hello. I'm Shirin. This is Roman. Thank you for joining us."

Roman joined the growing group, offering a rough hand for a shake. Roman moved like a soldier, but didn't put out any menace in that way some wannabe-alpha-types would to try to establish dominance.

"So where are we, exactly?"

Shirin said, "We're in the dimension of action narratives, in the region devoted to disaster narratives. How much did King explain?"

"Not much. I figured I would let you take this one." King crossed to the table with the computers, turning one to face him, revealing grainy footage of the entrance to a library.

"Several decades ago, the founders of the Genrenauts discovered that not only were there multiple dimensions, but every one beyond our own operated with different internal logics that line up with narrative genres. Worlds constantly playing out Romance stories or War stories, crime-ridden cities filled with hard-boiled detectives, femmes fatales, and so on."

Shirin walked Mallery over to the computer, where King was scanning through several video feeds. One showed the library entrance, another displayed the halls of a hospital with dozens of gurneys arrayed chaotically in every open space. "This world compares to movies like *The Andromeda Strain* or shows like *Designated Survivor*. There's a flu epidemic rippling across the city, and a terrorist cell that claims to have engineered the virus announced that they'd negotiate only with the mayor. Except the mayor has caught this flu and is in critical condition. That's where the story has gone wrong. That breach will create ripples to push the story farther off-course and cause more chaos."

Story worlds, broken stories. Okay, that's a lot.

"So what, the mayor looks enough like me that I'm your best match? Why me?"

"No, the mayor is fifty years old and five inches taller than you. We've got a device; consider it prosthetics. But that part is easy. Any of us could impersonate the mayor in theory, but this is the kind of role that is perfect for your talents."

Mallery sat back on her heels. "Hold on a minute. I was auditioning for *Mamma Mia* and now you want me to go into a hot zone and negotiate with a terrorist?"

"This is the job," King said. "It's dangerous, it's unpredictable, but it has as great an impact as you could ever hope for."

"And it pays incredibly well," Roman added.

Mallery cocked her head to the side. "No shit?"

Shirin said, "You could live on the Upper East Side."

Roman cut in, "But not really, since our team is based in Baltimore."

"You could live in Harbor East or Roland Park," King offered. "Here's the pitch. You come out with us and try this negotiation. Roman and Shirin will go with you, I'll be in your ear here. We have a backup plan if your conversation goes bad, and we've dealt with narrative breaches like this numerous times before. You go in and do your best, and we'll be there to do everything possible to give you what you need to succeed and a way out. If you need it."

She should just go home. Put all of this ridiculousness behind her, go back to grinding it out for the small roles, try to work her way up before she passed her Sell By date for ingénue roles and had to graduate to playing mothers and aunts and witches. Assuming she didn't get evicted first.

"If I screw up and people die, how am I supposed to live with that?"

Shirin extended a hand, pausing to let Mallery respond. She met it with her own. "If you can't handle that responsibility, this job is not for you. But if you succeed, if you join this team, you can save countless lives, all while having adventures and playing roles you could never imagine."

Mallery thought back to the first Broadway show she saw. She was seven years old, heartbroken by the death of the family cat, her first real experience with death and grief. They already had tickets to *Annie* and she'd thrown a fit, refusing to go, only relenting to the promise of ice cream after. She remembered seeing the little girl on stage not so much older than her. Seeing that girl tell the story of her own struggles, pouring her heart into song. And for a couple of hours, the passion of others had filled up that hole in her heart.

That night and every day since, she'd known that she wanted to do for others what that little girl and that show had done for her. Astronauts were out, Broadway was in.

Performance was just the means to the end of helping. Of staunching the wound, healing the pain.

This was a chance to do that in a bigger, scarier way than she'd ever imagined. And be an astronaut, too.

Mallery took a long breath and said, "Where's the footage for me to study?"

—

Mallery had taken some improv classes in college to push herself and round out her skill set in case her career path went in an unconventional direction.

This wasn't what she'd had in mind.

The character study parts were more familiar. Instead of a script or history books, she had several hours of video from this world's YouTube—campaign rallies and announcements mostly, with a few press briefings during crises, which proved the most instructive. Mayor Hughes had a tell when she was worried or stressed where she'd start more sentences with "So." She also adjusted her thick-rimmed black plastic glasses when she was gathering her thoughts to respond to a question.

Mallery took it all in, sketching notes by hand to help inscribe them on her mind, a trick she'd picked up in college when typing notes meant that everything went straight through her without setting up permanent shop. Mayor Hughes tended to sit back on her heels (wearing flats) unless challenged, where she'd shift forward and broaden her stance.

Vocally, the Mayor had a slightly rough alto voice and a Boston accent, which was thankfully easily within Mallery's range.

"Did you already know I could do the voice?" she asked as he stood beside her, Shirin and Roman off to one side preparing the outfits they were going to wear in to the negotiation.

"It's on your one-sheet. And before you ask, no, you weren't the only person I was there to see audition that day, though I already had my eye on you."

"I'm flattered. And slightly concerned. But that may be the fear talking. Did anyone else make the cut?"

The barest movement of one corner of a lip toward a smile. "Not yet."

Knowing there was competition just made Mallery more excited to succeed. It was, perhaps, not the best part of her personality, but you work with what God gave you.

Mallery cocked her head at something from a public address, then rolled it back to make sure she hadn't imagined it. That video clip led her back to the dossier. An angle started coming into shape.

"So, I've got a pitch for another approach here."

———

Twenty minutes later, King checked his watch. "Ready or not, it's time to go. Mayor's office just finalized the meet. Shirin has your wardrobe."

Shirin held up a dark blue suit and a grey shell top and an equally pair of boring black flats. Absolute garbage outfit. "Yes, it's horrid. But this is what she wears. I do need to know whether you can keep yourself from fussing with your hair. Mayor Hughes has a pixie cut and if you're fussing with hair that shouldn't exist, we'll need to get you into a wig. Which would not be fun to do in a car."

"I'm good. I've locked in three distinct ticks from the footage, and none of them involve hair."

"Good. We're out the door in five."

———

Mallery had to look away from the streets. Emergency vehicles, fires, even a stand-off with police.

This wasn't real-life disaster, where most people stayed home if they could or went to lend a helping hand. This was movie disaster, where everyone lost their cool all at once and started looting and fleeing or looting while fleeing.

The glasses were prescription-free, so all they did was serve as a prop for one of the ticks she'd selected for the performance.

Beside her, Shirin wore a charcoal-grey suit, her hair tied up and back into a bun. She looked like any of a thousand middle-aged political aides. Roman had a rougher look, a well-worn suit with an armpit holster. All three of them wore medical-grade masks.

"There's a bag full of guns in the car's trunk. In case things break really bad," Roman said as they drove. Which wasn't remotely reassuring. But something about how Roman moved told her that Roman could handle himself if it came to a fight.

King came through the in-ear comms Shirin had distributed to the team. "The terrorist leader has identified himself only as Omega. As far as we can tell, his people are mostly ex-military and/or rejects from local police academy. Several white supremacist connections, but our operations handler is running down the specifics."

Mallery revised her estimation of Omega from terrible to absolute evil.

"Does the actual mayor know what you're doing?" Mallery asked.

Shirin said, "The deputy mayor is our contact. They think we're a federal crisis response team."

Mallery cocked her head. "That doesn't make a lot of sense?"

King in her ear again. "When a story breach starts rippling, the world becomes more eager to correct itself. If you're working to get things back on track, these kinds of con jobs are easier. Plus, we have established aliases in this region from previous missions."

"What has Omega been asking for and what terms can I reasonably offer?"

"He's looking for prisoner releases and a state-level bill declaring the white race officially superior in the eyes of the state."

Mallery exhaled a long breath. She was in the extremely deep end now. "Yikes. Even more horrible if we're talking about other white supremacist prisoners. What if I just keep him talking and that gives the SWAT team time to come in and shoot everyone? Can we just do that?"

"We can, but it is dangerous. Our projections give us a much higher risk of someone getting shot if we move for endgame immediately."

"What's the play?"

"Initial negotiations, promise that you'll speak with the governor and president about their demands, then we take the information from your meeting about how many people Omega has and where to the SWAT team and they make their plan to get in and rescue the hostages."

"Promise nothing solid, probe for information, and get out quickly? Sounds like my Friday nights trolling for dates on @_personals_."

No response.

"Do any of you date much?"

Shirin shrugged. "I've been married for over a decade."

"Not really," Roman said.

"No comment," King added.

"Nevermind, then. Pretend I just said 'I can do that.' and let's move on without me having to drag myself more than I already have."

"We're coming up on the library. I'll park a block away and walk us in. King, give me whatever sightlines you can access through the cameras."

Shirin handed Mallery a three-inch-wide disk with a button in the middle and a glowing screen. "Here's your Phase Manipulator. It'll make you look like the Mayor. Don't touch or fiddle with it, just leave it in the pocket of the suit."

"I don't want to ask how this works, do I?"

"No. We don't have the time. Just pretend it doesn't exist, and stay in character until told otherwise."

The car slowed and pulled into an open spot, a car on fire three spots down.

"Everyone out of the car and form up on me in three."

"Okay, really, wow," Mallery said, her heart racing like she'd heard a thousand pairs of hands applauding the curtain draw.

"Just stick with us," Shirin said.

"Two."

Mallery unbuckled the seatbelt and took a breath, then got out of the car, falling into step behind Roman, who moved with fluid power.

"Just look forward," she told herself, focusing on Roman's form through the echoes of gunshots, fire, and screams.

Was this world like this all the time? Just one disaster after another, terrorists around every corner? Like daytime Fox News come to life?

King came in through the comms. "Turn right at this corner, then the library entrance is at the center of the block."

Roman turned the corner and immediately dove for cover.

"Contact left high!" he shouted, rolling up into a ready position behind a van. He reached out and grabbed Mallery, pulling her beside him. "Stay down. Shirin, arc out and see if you can cover me."

"How is she going to move to cover you in this?" Bullets shredded the other side of the car, shattering glass and piercing metal.

"Turtle crawl?" Shirin suggested.

"No, just trust me," Mallery said. She adjusted her glasses to ground herself, then stepped into the spotlight, projecting her character voice. "This is Mayor Young! I'm here to negotiate with Omega! Cease fire and let us approach or you get nothing!"

The gunfire kept coming. "I really wish you hadn't." Roman

no-look fired, then signaled Mallery to follow him to the next vehicle and leave behind the ruined van.

Mallery wanted to curl up and pretend none of this was happening, but Mayor Hughes was a combat veteran and "never backed down from a fight." Mallery took another deep breath and shouted. "If you keep shooting at us, you get nothing, you hear that? Cease fire immediately and we talk about what we can do so everyone wins."

"Back her play," King said over comms.

A tinny voice blasted from the library's PA.

"Let the Mayor in."

The gunfire stopped a few seconds later.

Roman waited a beat more, then stood, gun still ready but down. "Okay, we're good." Roman led the three of them down the street, calling out locations of three different gunners in a low voice.

"You're doing great so far, Mallery. Keep it rolling. Don't try to go too heavy on them, but stay strong."

There were two gunmen at the front entrance of the library, wearing a mix of camo and tacticool gear and inexplicably, one Greek-style pauldron per person.

Mallery didn't have time to take in the décor as the gunmen led them through a side door, up some stairs, and around a switchback to a lushly-appointed office with bookshelves across one wall and windows overlooking a reading room on the other. Inside was Omega, looking a bit more haggard than the intelligence shots in his packet. But that haggardness came with a hungry look. His movements were sharp, almost excessive, like he had too much strength and had to pull back. He gestured to a chair opposite him at a massive oak desk. He was, of course, not wearing a mask.

"Madam Mayor. Soo kind of you to finally show up."

She pulled off her mask, step one of her plan. "I've got a few things on my plate at the moment."

"Not my problem."

"It is, though. You cannot expect me to pretend that nothing else is happening in my city or that you're not responsible for keeping me from getting here earlier. I appreciate that your people and your agenda come first, but if we're to reach an understanding, we have to approach this collaboratively."

"Good," King said on comms. "Keep him on the back foot if you can, and move to gathering information."

Omega picked up his weapon, leading to a classic "everyone points guns at everyone moment".

Mallery slowly raised a hand to adjust her glasses, rooting herself in character, willing herself steady. "If we're all bleeding out on this nice carpet, no one wins. Tell me what you want and how you'd like to get out of my city. Because no matter what we agree on, you're not staying. Doesn't help me continue my work, if you understand."

Omega grinned like a cat spying a flightless bird. "First, release Justinian Dei and the captive members of Populous Vult. Then you'll issue a mayoral decree in support of the superiority of the white race, and you're going to give us five million dollars and a fully-fueled freight ship that will be unimpeded when we leave the city with our fellow warriors."

"Good," King said on comms. "Draw out any other information you can, then we can get you out of there."

"That's the kind of clear communication I was hoping to hear."

And here's where Mallery played her ace. She'd noticed little indicators here and there and put it all together while watching a speech from a year back when Mayor Hughes had briefly flashed the OK symbol with one hand while talking about police accountability.

"I knew you were someone we could reason with. I've read your manifestos, you know. Homeland and heritage are very important to me."

The words were acid on her tongue, but this was the job. If she could convince him she was receptive, he might tip his hand. Mallery might not get the science fiction part of this, but she knew stories, and she knew people.

Growing up Jewish with grandparents who had survived the Holocaust, she was exceedingly vigilant about dog whistles. Which led her to forums and conspiracy theories that Mayor Hughes was secretly a white nationalist. Mallery had learned to vet people after dating a crypto-fascist in college.

Omega tried to keep a poker face, but she saw the fire of self-righteousness zealotry burn across his face beyond his control. "Maybe we can make a deal."

"So, the declaration I can make tonight. But I need a show of cooperation from you to sell this to the public. I've worked long and hard to advocate for my beliefs in this city, I trust you'll understand what it has taken to bend the system to my will. Release a third of the hostages—the pregnant, the elderly, the ill. I can have the ship ready by midnight. The prisoner release depends on the Governor."

Omega started pacing, excited. The guards seemed to relax, as if they recognized this mode.

King on comms again. "You've got him hooked. Here's the opening for the next story beat. Roman, you're on."

The team's heavy sprung into motion. Two silenced shots rang out and the guards were down before Mallery could blink. Roman was on Omega, spinning him and wrapping his arms around the terrorist's neck. Omega gasped, flailed for his gun, then went limp.

All of that in a matter of seconds.

"Good job," Roman said to Mallery. "And good plan. You ready for the next part?"

This involved Shirin impersonating Omega with her PPM and ordering the terrorists to release hostages, then depart, claiming victory. The boat waiting for the terrorists led directly into a trap.

Mallery took a few minutes to let the nerves shake out while Shirin changed. The older woman adjusted her wardrobe and hair to fit

Omega's look, then activated her PPM to take on the form of Omega. It was unnervingly accurate. Roman took the clothes from one of the guards, pulled the bandana up over his nose, and then set his PPM on one of the dead guards, changing them to look like Roman. Then Roman grabbed the guard's gun, hauled the dead Roman-but-not guard up onto his shoulder, and set up position behind the other two.

Shirin took command of the situation and led the three of them out, immediately shouting at the guards to shape up.

Mallery stayed in character as they left. The terrorists cheered the concessions promised by her as the mayor. Omega's people released the hostages at the dock, the chunk of hostages and as Roman and Shirin arranged for Mallery to be led out back to her car. Roman rejoined her minutes later, leaving Shirin to execute the rest of the plan.

"You've done more than enough," Roman's voice rang in her ear. "Get back here and you'll get to watch as we wrap this up."

———

Mallery was surprised to find that she was more nervous when she was outside the action looking in. She stood, glued to camera feeds of Shirin-as-Omega gathering the terrorists to "receive their brethren" when in fact Roman and King were coordinating with the local SWAT team to systematically remove the terrorists once they were exposed at the port. Meanwhile, as the situation grew dire for the terrorists, Shirin pulled a vanish, leaving them without their leader.

And just like that, it was done. Shirin returned to the warehouse while Roman and King cleaned up, made notes for re-supply (a task Mallery was happy to help with because it let her poke and prod at all of the different facets of the job), and when Shirin sank into a chair, King produced a flask and handed out small tin cups.

"Team tradition. We work together, we celebrate together. Today, you were part of the team. Tomorrow, that's up to you."

Mallery took the offered cup, smelled the peaty rich caramel liquor pouring from the flask, and thought about what the future offered. An endless supply of all-engrossing roles, an end to the grind, and a chance to keep dreaming this wild dream.

"To another happy ending," King said. The four raised their cups as one.

"To the future," Mallery added, her decision made. Mallery was born for show business, but it turned out her real stage was much bigger than she'd ever imagined.

Michael R. Underwood is an author, podcaster, and publishing professional. His books include space opera *Annihilation Aria*, the Ree Reyes *Geekomancy* books, the Stabby Award finalist *Genrenauts* series, and *Born to the Blade* (written with Malka Older, Cassandra Khaw, and Marie Brennan). He's been a bookseller, sales representative, and was the North American Sales & Marketing Manager for Angry Robot Books. He is also a co-host of the actual play show Speculate! and a guest host on the Hugo Award-finalist The Skiffy and Fanty Show.

Mike lives in Baltimore with his wife, their dog, and an ever-growing library. When not writing, he geeks out with games and makes pizzas from scratch.

Gallery

R. L. King

Tanner Lowe always found a brisk, late-night walk did wonders for taking the edge off his buzz.

He ambled along, hands in his pockets, whistling an off-key rendition of one of the pounding dance tunes that had been shaking the walls at the party he'd just left.

Xi Delta Mu put on the best bashes, which was the main reason Tanner made a point to show up to them. You could count on the Xi-Delts for the best booze, the best weed, and above all, the best chicks.

That last one had definitely been true tonight. Tanner smiled, picturing the pretty sophomore's face as she lay sprawled across the bed in some anonymous bro's room. He didn't know her name and didn't care, but the way her long, surfer-blond hair had spread over the pillow, the way her bright-red lipstick had smeared when he kissed her, the way she'd mumbled half-hearted protests at him as he fumbled at her spaghetti-strap tank top—all of those were sure-fire ways to get his engine running.

Oh, yeah, she'd wanted him. He'd had no doubt of it. He'd watched her for most of the night, and didn't miss the way she'd smiled at him as she finished beer after beer, laughing with her friends, fearless and carefree the way all sorority chicks were. He'd always been good at knowing when to make his move, and this had been no exception. She wouldn't remember a thing in the morning.

And even if she did, she'd never be able to prove it. He'd just make a quick call to Dad, and the magic lawyers would make it all go away.

His father might grumble a little, but he'd do it. Because he knew how these things worked, and because Tanner was certain he'd indulged in the same thing on more than one occasion when he'd been in college.

Damn, it was good to be young, hot, and rich.

The walk back to his own frat house was about a mile, and took him along a side street lined with small storefront businesses. He frowned when he spotted lights on in one of them. There weren't any bars or restaurants here, so this time of night they should all be closed up tight.

Ah, well. He didn't care why some mom-and-pop shop had its lights on this late. All he wanted to do now was get home, climb into bed, and spend a little quality time replaying this evening's activities.

As he drew closer, he slowed.

That was weird.

The place had a pair of picture windows on either side of an old-fashioned door. One contained a large painting on an antique easel, the other a sculpture on a pedestal. Subtle lights illuminated each. Tanner looked for a business name above the door, but didn't see one. He didn't see an address number, either.

He definitely would have noticed an art gallery before, though.

Maybe it was new.

Despite his intention to continue past the place and get home, something in the painting and the sculpture drew his eye. Both were of an abstract style—the painting in jagged brushstrokes of red, purple, and black, the sculpture a writhing gray mass of what looked like worms or snakes.

"Badass ..." he muttered. One of those bad boys would look great in his room, not to mention impressing the guys. Nearly before he realized what he was doing, he tried the door.

It opened easily. Somewhere in the back, a bell tinkled.

Tanner stepped inside. Most of his buzz had departed by now. He supposed he could spare a few minutes to check out this odd place.

He'd taken in only a quick impression of a room with a polished wood floor, doorways leading off in three directions, and white walls, when a pleasant voice called to him from somewhere to his left.

"Good evening! Welcome. It's a pleasure to have you here."

Tanner spun.

The person who'd entered through the shadowy left-side doorway was a woman, but nobody could fault Tanner for briefly thinking otherwise. Her hair, almost unnaturally white-blond, was done in a short undercut, and a sweeping, knee-length cutaway coat of deep maroon, trim black trousers, and a vest of lighter red covered her slim, boyish frame. Her eyes, brilliant emerald green in a pale face, followed him with amusement. Tanner rarely attended his English classes and even more rarely did the assignments, but if he had, the adjective "elfin" might have come to mind.

"Welcome to my gallery," the woman said again. "I'm glad you've stopped by. Please feel free to look around. We've got a fresh new collection, so you'll be the first to see some of them."

"Thanks." He aimed his best seductive smile at her—the one he could almost always count on to get him laid. Not that he had that on his mind now, of course—this chick would definitely look a lot hotter if she wore a little makeup and didn't dress like a dude—but it had become almost a reflex around anyone female.

"Oh, I probably would," she agreed brightly. "And if that mattered to me in the slightest, I might even consider it."

He gaped at her, wondering if he'd somehow spoken the words aloud instead of thinking them. But before he could reply, she spread her arms, encompassing the area around her. "Please, though—take a look around. I'm certain you'll find at least a few things to your liking."

"Uh. Yeah." He struggled to regain his composure. "I did like that stuff in your front windows."

"Thank you. Those are two of my favorites."

"What kind of gallery is this, anyway?"

"Oh, a bit of this, a bit of that," she said with an airy wave. "Come on—since you're our first visitor, I'll give you the tour."

He was beginning to think his smartest decision would be to get the hell out of here and get home, but something about the woman intrigued him. Maybe he'd let her show him around for a little while and then make an excuse to clear out.

He followed her through the doorway into the next room. It remained dark until they'd passed the threshold, then unseen lights came up to illuminate a space fifteen feet on a side, with the same light-wood floor and stark white walls as the front room. This time, two doorways led off into other darkened spaces.

Only a single piece occupied the room—a painting in an ornate frame, hanging on the opposite wall from the doorway where they'd entered.

Normally, Tanner Lowe was a young man of big gestures and loud voice, taking up his share of space in the world and more because he'd been raised to believe he deserved to. Now, though, something about this painting made him hesitate as he approached it.

It wasn't as big as the one in the front window. Composed of sharp lines and discordant angles, it depicted a wide, fleshy face with brush-cut hair and staring eyes. Its open mouth was a black maw that seemed almost to stretch behind the painting, as if inviting Tanner to stick his fist into it. Behind the face, a line of smaller figures stretched out in the distance, their height increasing from small ones to the left to taller ones on the right. All of them were watching the open-mouthed man in the foreground.

Something squirmed in the pit of Tanner's stomach. The image wasn't moving—that would be crazy—but the way the brushstrokes had been applied gave him the impression that it was.

A small, gold plate on the bottom of the frame read simply, *Tormentor. Timothy Miller, 1974.*

The man in the painting certainly didn't look like a tormentor. If anything, he looked torment*ed*. Tanner swallowed and pointed at the plate. "Is that the artist?"

"In a way, I suppose it is." She still sounded as if the whole world amused her. "Shall we continue? We don't have the whole collection in yet, but there's still quite a lot to see." She indicated the doorway to the right.

The lights came up on a new room. Same size, same wood floor, same white walls—but this one had doorways exiting to three sides instead of two, and the single piece here was a sculpture on a pedestal in the center.

Something in the far reaches of Tanner's mind poked at him. The storefront he'd seen from the street had been quite small, with other closed businesses on either side. How did this place possibly have the space for this many rooms with only one exhibit each? *Eh. Probably some trick of space. Or else those shops on either side are false fronts.* Whatever it was, he didn't much care.

Once again, the smiling gallery owner remained discreetly in the doorway, allowing Tanner the freedom to examine the room's piece on his own.

The sculpture, carved from a black substance with red veins running through it, showed the full-sized torsos and heads of two peo-ple—a balding man in his forties and a girl in her middle teens. The style was different this time, not as abstract as the painting but still strange and distinctly alien. The man faced away from the girl, his expression haunted, his mouth agape, his hands reaching out in a pleading gesture. Behind him, the girl was smiling.

The plate attached to the pedestal read, *Stepfather. Ralph Abrams, 1993.*

Tanner's stomach squirmed again, and he turned away. "You know, these are great, but I should be getting back. I'm pretty tired and I have a paper due on Monday I haven't started yet."

The proprietor chuckled. "Just a few more, I promise. I've got a couple coming up I think you'll really like. But if you'd rather go, I understand. Some people simply can't handle this kind of unconventional art. It's nothing to be ashamed of."

Tanner glared. Was she calling him scared? He towered at least six inches over her, and outweighed her by more than fifty pounds. If he wanted to, he could teach her a thing or two about being scared.

She was watching him now, with that same enigmatic grin and her arms crossed. If she'd caught anything of his thoughts this time, she showed no sign of it. She seemed to be waiting for him to decide which way he wanted to take this.

The anger surged, but he shoved it down. "Fine," he muttered. "Let's see the rest. And maybe I can talk to you about buying that one in the front window."

"Oh, no. I'm afraid that's not possible. None of the pieces here are for sale."

He grunted, but didn't otherwise reply. Maybe when he called his father tomorrow, he'd see if he could change that. Everything—and everybody—had a price. That was another thing Dad had taught him.

"Shall we continue?" The proprietor gestured toward another doorway.

Tanner lost track of time as the strange, cheerful woman led him from one room to the next. Some of the exhibits were paintings, some sculptures, some mixed-media pieces—there was even a series of several black-and-white photographs depicting a man whose face appeared to be melting off. Each one included a title, a name, and a date. The dates spanned over a hundred years, beginning in the early part of the last century. The most recent one, a screaming woman rendered in childlike, colorful fingerpaints, was named *Mother, Michelle LaRue*, and dated last year. By the time the proprietor paused before leaving that room, Tanner's mouth had gone dry, his stomach roiling with either unease or too much beer, or maybe both.

He decided he did *not* want to ask Dad to try convincing her to sell him the painting from the front window.

"Look," he said, not even caring if the woman thought he was the world's biggest coward, "I need to go. I don't feel so good." He flashed her a self-deprecating grin. "Too much partying, I guess. You know how it is."

She smiled. "I completely understand. But before you go, I've got one more exhibit you must see. It's right up ahead here, and I guarantee it will speak to you. I've saved it for last for just that reason. Would you indulge me, this one time? It's on the way out."

By now, the seemingly random route through different directions of doorways had thoroughly disoriented Tanner, to the point where he wasn't sure he could find his way out on his own. Not that he'd ever admit that, of course. "Sure, whatever. One more. But then I'm outta here."

"I promise. One more." She gestured toward the doorway directly in front of them. Like all the others, the space beyond it was wreathed in shadow. "You go on ahead. I've got something I need to attend to, and in any case this one is best experienced solo. I'll be right back!"

Sudden panic gripped him. He wanted to yell, "No! Don't go!" He wanted to grab her by the arm and force her to stay. But of course he didn't do either of those things. Even now, his lifelong conditioning held. There was no way in hell he was going to let this woman think he was a wimp.

He turned around to tell her he was fine.

The doorway was empty. She had already slipped away.

He paused a moment, taking a couple of deep breaths. Warmth prickled his cheeks. *Come on, you wuss. They're just paintings. Look at one more and you can go home and think about the good parts of tonight. Maybe if the hot blond girl didn't remember him, he might have another shot at her next time.*

Smiling at the thought, he straightened his jacket and strode through the doorway. He was Tanner Martin Lowe the Third, and one more creepy painting wasn't going to freak him out. He'd tell Dad about this place when he called tomorrow, and they'd both have a good laugh about it.

Like all the other rooms he'd visited, this one was dark. This time, though, the lights didn't come up immediately. He paused in the center and held his hand up in front of him, but couldn't see it.

"Hello?"

The lights switched on.

This room had the same pale wood floor and white walls as all the others. It was the same size—fifteen feet on a side. But this time, it didn't have any other exits.

The canvas on the opposite wall, hung within a geometric frame of burnished bronze, was blank.

For a moment, Tanner thought the frame was empty, enclosing part of the wall in some kind of pretentious artistic "statement." But as he drew closer, he discovered he was wrong. The canvas was there, as white and pristine as the wall behind it, as if waiting for someone to come along and do something about it.

What the hell?

Was this some kind of joke?

He looked over his shoulder, back through the doorway—but now that space was as dark as the interior of this room had been a moment ago.

"This is some messed-up shit," he muttered.

He turned back to face the canvas. He hadn't noticed before, but it had a little plate attached below the frame, just like all the other ones had. He bent to read it.

Predator. Tanner Lowe, 2022.

When the gallery's proprietor returned ten minutes later, she smiled in satisfaction.

She crossed the room and paused in front of the canvas. No longer blank, it now featured a handsome, dark-haired young man, his mouth open in a jaw-cracking scream. His gaze, wide-eyed and terrified, met hers, but she paid him no mind. Behind him, a number of other figures with long hair and pretty faces gathered on either side, their smiles as sharp as knives, their eyes glittering with possibility. The harsh, red-and-black brushstrokes gave way here to richer colors: deep blues, golds, purples, greens.

The proprietor's smile broadened, and her bright, emerald eyes twinkled with mirth. She raised a feather duster, gave the painting an insouciant little swipe, then turned smartly and left the room, whistling the tune from Tanner's party.

The light went out as she exited, plunging the room back into darkness.

But when she paused and listened closely, she could still hear him screaming.

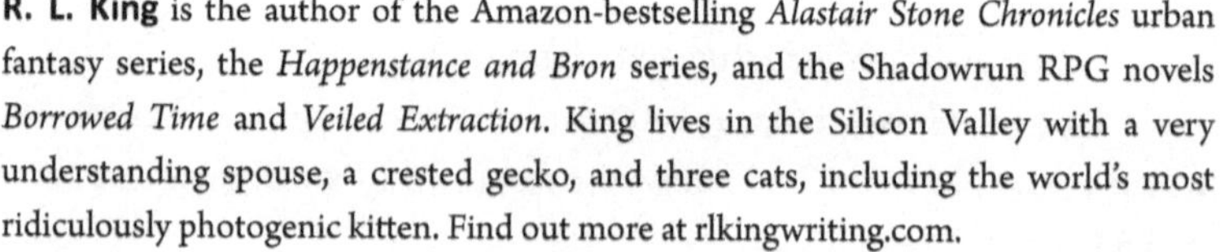

R. L. King is the author of the Amazon-bestselling *Alastair Stone Chronicles* urban fantasy series, the *Happenstance and Bron* series, and the Shadowrun RPG novels *Borrowed Time* and *Veiled Extraction*. King lives in the Silicon Valley with a very understanding spouse, a crested gecko, and three cats, including the world's most ridiculously photogenic kitten. Find out more at rlkingwriting.com.

Butterflies Through the Gray

Addie J. King

GRAY. Everything around me was gray.

The sky was gray. The clouds were gray. The walls on the side of my apartment building were gray. It seemed like I was walking through a cloud of varying shades of gray.

It matched my mood. Ever since last Christmas, I hadn't even had enough of a mood to add any sort of color to my life.

I hadn't painted. I hadn't picked up my sketchbook. Yesterday, I'd tried to sit down at my desk, and I couldn't even bring myself to pick up a pencil. And the grayness just continued to grow, until it seemed like I was wrapped in a gray cloud, barely walking through the world.

It had been that way since I lost my sister, just six weeks ago.

Each step was harder and harder, and only knowing that I didn't have a choice kept me going down the sidewalk to the corner store. My glasses fogged from my breath leaking up under my mask, further graying my vision.

I knew I needed to go to the store. I knew I needed to buy food, but nothing sounded good, nothing made me feel hungry. I forced myself to push the door open at the local shop, going inside. I stood in front of the cooler, looking at the drinks that should have been brightly colored and almost garish, and they barely registered in my sight. I pulled a bottle of water from the cooler, knowing I needed to get something to drink, and almost put it back. Not even water sounded good.

I trudged back towards the entrance and grabbed a shopping basket. There wasn't much to eat in the house. I knew I'd been losing weight, and I hadn't been grocery shopping. Anything still in my house had gone bad weeks ago. I knew I had to eat something.

I had to stop and sit down at the bench just inside the doors. I was already exhausted, and I hadn't finished shopping yet. I used to run every morning. Now, walking two blocks to the store and looking at a bottle of water had worn me out.

Why couldn't I be more like Elsie? I wondered, missing her so badly it hurt.

Just six weeks ago, I'd lost her. Elizabeth Simmons, to her adoring public, Elsie to me. She'd been my older sister, my mentor, my friend, my world. Six years older than me, she was a force of nature, and I'd always been happy to just absorb the energy she gave off. I'd been following her and her friends around since we were little. She'd been an amazing artist, and I'd followed her to art school. She'd sold her sculptures and statutes all over the world for the last few years. I'd followed her around from art show to gallery to fancy restaurant to dinner party for years. She'd been a world-renowned artist, an outgoing bubbly personality. The media loved her. Art critics loved her. She'd been an international star, with some of her figures selling for huge money, the smooth curving of the stone she worked with prized in some of the biggest art sales in the last ten years.

And she was gone. And so was all the color in the world.

I still remembered dropping her off at the hospital, her labored breathing scaring me. She hadn't wanted to go to the hospital, with all the scary stuff on the news, but I insisted. She'd been as strong as a horse, in the shape of her life, and now she was winded just getting out of the cab at the hospital. She'd been sick for five days before I'd insisted that she go in.

She died five days later, intubated, her own lungs working against her.

I'd suffered at home, a mild case of coronavirus, recovering with no major lasting symptoms, barely a cough for three days. I'd lost my sense of taste and smell and those were still barely starting to come back. It had made my sense of grayness worse. My last conversation with my sister was over a video chat, her barely able to whisper my name.

I felt the grayness close over me again, a pain in my heart from her not sitting next to me pointing out color and light and shadow, even in a boring old neighborhood mom and pop shop. But the grayness also kept the sadness from taking over. All the color and light had gone out of the world, and I couldn't even bring myself to have enough energy to cry.

I stared down at the dirty vinyl flooring in the store. Mrs. James, the shopkeeper I'd known since Elsie and I had moved to the neighborhood four years ago, came up beside me and laid one hand on her shoulder. "My dear, we all miss her. Please know we are all thinking about you." The hand left my shoulder, and I felt the warmth it had left. It had been so long since anyone had touched me. The distancing and the stay-at-home orders and then quarantine had me so disconnected from anything resembling reality. Even Elsie had grown quieter before she got sick. That vibrant larger than life personality had faded from week after week of being away from her fans, her critics, and the endless socializing she'd thrived in.

That warmth on my shoulder was like a tiny ray of sunshine that I felt burrow its way into my soul. I looked up and saw Mrs. James, standing six feet away; I tried to smile in a way that she would be able to see it in my eyes, since the smile would be covered by the mask across my face.

"We all miss her, dear. Oh, I hate all this. I just want to give you a big hug!" she exclaimed and threw her arms open.

I started to run towards her, but I couldn't do it. Something held me back. But even as I was trying to will my limbs into moving towards her, I saw her face fall and her arms drop. "It's okay. We're distancing, too," she said, in a hopeless voice.

I felt the gray move back into place, as the sunbeam warmth began to fade. And Mrs. James' small granddaughters peeked around her legs, wearing pink and purple face masks with small, embroidered butterflies tucked on the far-right side of their masks. I stared at the butterflies, and for some reason they seemed to grow and nearly leap off the cloth, which grayed out behind the color of the blue and pink and purple butterfly wings.

Time stood still as the butterflies appeared to jump off the girls' masks and twirl their way around me. I stopped looking at the gray and followed the butterfly wings instead as they twirled around my head. I stopped being stuck in the gray long enough to watch the dance of the butterflies, worried where they could go in the world of gray, and then realized that the gray had receded enough that it didn't block their path.

My fingers began to itch. I wanted to recreate those butterflies, because of their colorful escape for me. They were an escape from the gray, from the silence in my head. I wanted to have their shape and color fill my soul, and to fill the soul of others. I felt them fill me up, a rainbow of relief filling my cells and the marrow of my bones.

It was the essence of life, bringing back to me the idea of life as an interaction with others, a connection born of perfection, an interaction of the soul.

I stood up, and ran through the shelves in the small store, grabbing pasta and sauce and garlic and mushrooms, and hurrying home to create a dish that could warm in the slow cooker while I worked. I got home and browned some pork that had been in the freezer, added the mushrooms that I'd grabbed that day. I mixed up a hearty tomato and meat sauce and made enough pasta, in salty, starchy water, that I had enough in meals for a few days, warmed for when I was ready to eat.

And then I got to work.

I found myself drawing again, fascinated by the butterfly wings and the colors I'd just seen after months and weeks of nothing but gray.

I ate quickly, spaghetti and sauce in a bowl Elsie had thrown when she had dabbled in pottery as I stared at canvases, looking for the next angle, the next shadow, the next light. I ate in between stretches of mad painting, adding shading and color and highlights and shadow and fighting with daylight for the right light to illuminate my soul. It felt like someone was tapping me on the shoulder to remind me to eat, so fevered was my need to capture those butterflies.

I drank nothing but water; tasteless, colorless, and only when it felt like someone was putting a bottle in my hand.

I realized at one point that it did feel like someone was actually putting the water bottle in my hand, even though I remembered filling it up a few times. But no one else lived with me, and no one else could understand that feeling—that I was not creating alone.

Three days later, I had multiple canvases around the loft, with varying scenes of the butterflies I'd seen. I'd been painting in a mad fever, and I had paint everywhere. I was exhausted, but color was seeping back into my world. I saw the blues and pinks and purples merging on the canvas to show a lifting of the spirit in my paintings.

I sat down heavily on the futon in the studio of our apartment; it was an old warehouse that Elsie had bought before the pandemic. We'd made the open floor area our studio, since there were so many large windows to let in the light. We'd converted the offices off to the side into our bedrooms, the kitchen, and the bathroom. I glanced over at the closed door of her room and sighed. I knew that one day I'd have to go in there, I'd have to go through her things and figure out how to take apart the life she had built. I knew she had a few pieces that she had been working on just before she went to the hospital, and I wondered if she had been able to finish them; she had quarantined in her room when she had tested positive for the virus.

Later, I promised myself. A few things needed to be taken care of first.

I took a shower, and washed my hair. I guzzled a cold bottle of water, the last one in the refrigerator. I put on clean clothes that weren't pajamas or a bathrobe and put on makeup as a pick me up. I took the time to style my hair, and felt more like myself than I had for a while.

I picked up my cell phone and ordered a pizza. I'd run through the small amount of food I'd bought, and I was starving, but the spices and taste of Italian food had started to cut through the lack of taste I'd had for weeks, so I figured I'd stick with what was working. While I waited for the delivery guy, I started to clean my brushes, and put away the paint, going through the familiar motions of the actions I used to do daily. I'd always painted, but Elsie had been the star. I had a whole stack of paintings in one corner of our studio, that I'd never shown anyone. I painted while she sculpted, and we'd always worked together, but no matter how much she had begged me to show my work, I never did. I had been content to live in her shadow, but that shadow didn't exist any longer.

The buzzer rang. I'd paid for the pizza on their app, so I was able to look out of the keyhole and see that the delivery boy had left it on the small wrought iron table we'd set outside for exactly that reason at the beginning of the pandemic. I brought in the pizza and called one of Elsie's gallery owner friends.

"Mona, how are you doing?" I asked when she answered the phone.

"Abigail!" She exclaimed; the surprise evident in her voice. "I heard about Elsie, I'm more worried about you. No one has heard from you in weeks. Are you okay?"

I smiled. Part of the problem lately is that I hadn't even felt like being on social media, I hadn't video chatted with any of my friends, and I hadn't attended any of Elsie's Zoom classes, where she'd been teaching sculpting techniques for the last six months while we'd all been trying to work from home. Those classes had just abruptly stopped, and I'd leaned on Mona and some of Elsie's other friends to spread the word and help me deal with the details of refunds and such after Elsie's death. "I'm okay. Today is better. It's been rough."

Mona had been like an honorary aunt to the two of us; we didn't have much family other than each other and it sure had seemed like I was alone when I lost Elsie. "I've been so worried about you. Have you recovered okay? From the virus, I mean."

"As far as I can tell, I have. Taste and smell are just starting to come back. I still get tired, but I went out to the store for food yesterday, and I just got a pizza. I can taste the pepperoni." It tasted *good. Sooooo good.* I chewed on another piece as we talked, knowing it was rude, but I knew I needed the calories. Mona would understand. I'd be surprised if she didn't show up with food to make sure I would eat.

"I know it hasn't been very long, but we've gotten the details on Elsie's online classes all tied up. I have all the records when it's time to deal with that, but otherwise, are you okay?"

Elsie had been very successful. The warehouse was paid for, the bills weren't bad. I had been her power of attorney, her assistant, and her sole beneficiary. I didn't really have to worry about money for a while, but eventually I would need to do something to support myself. "I'm okay at the moment, but Mona, the reason I'm calling is that I think I'm ready to show someone some paintings."

Mona had been asking to see paintings of mine for years. I strongly suspected that Elsie had shown them to her behind my back, but neither of them had ever admitted it.

"Oh, I'd love to see them. Can I come right over?" she asked, the excitement so strong I could reach out and touch it. Maybe they hadn't conspired to see them when I was gone after all.

I laughed. "If you want to." I'd had the virus, and the news said I had some immunity now, but I'd wear a mask, and I was sure she would too. Someday they might approve the vaccine that I kept hearing about on the news. I'd be the first in line to get it if I could. I didn't want to die like my sister, and I didn't want anyone else to die like that either. I didn't know how long I might be safe and did not want to get it again.

The warehouse was big enough to be apart from each other, and I really did think I was ready to hear what she thought, especially on these paintings. I'd open some of the big windows for air circulation like the news told us to do. For some reason I didn't have the normal reluctance I used to have. It was as if I was being encouraged somehow to do this. If I didn't know better, I'd say it was Elsie pushing me to go forward. I took a deep breath. "I think I'm finally ready to do this."

Mona showed up within an hour. "Sorry it took so long to get here. I couldn't talk Paul into staying at home. He's in the car, dying of curiosity to see your paintings, but I made him promise that he had to stay in the car unless you were okay with him coming in."

I laughed, feeling more lightness and joy than I had in a long time. I was starting to notice the colors of our studio again, the cowhide chair Elsie liked to lounge on when she took a break from a large sculpture, the bright pink futon across from it where I would crash after a long stretch of painting. I could see the green on the leaves of the trees outside of the windows. "Of course, Paul can look as well. I'm curious about what you might think of them. I haven't painted since before she got sick. It felt like I had to paint these. I don't have her here for input."

They came in, masked with black cloth masks with the logo of their shared gallery on the front. I knew it was them, from their eyes, but I wasn't used to seeing either of them in jeans, or with the masks. I was more used to seeing them at gallery shows, or fancy dinner parties. It was familiar but strange at the same time. I could almost consider them strangers looking at my art, and I felt the familiar tug to hide my work, as I also felt a strange compulsion to shrug that off. That was new.

I showed them in and offered them bottles of water. They declined and headed straight for the center of the studio. Five paintings were set up on easels or leaned against chairs I'd brought in for the purpose, to display each of them in the room, in a circle, where someone in the center could slowly turn and catch each of them and take them in as a group. I'd seen that done before with Elsie's sculptures in their gallery.

Mona and Paul exchanged looks that I couldn't decipher. They were silent as I stood there watching them, waiting for a reaction, chewing on my lower lip under my mask.

A full ten minutes went by, with no reaction. I was starting to think they were trying to figure out how to tell me that the paintings sucked, the reaction I was so worried for years that I would get if I showed anyone my work.

I could hear the ticking of the clock in the corner, and the gray started to come back in, but I felt a shove from behind, almost like Elsie used to do on the playground when we were in elementary school, to get me, the shy younger sister, to join in a game or to climb on the monkey bars with everyone else. It felt like she was right there with me. I hoped that feeling never went away.

"Abigail," Mona breathed. "They are breathtaking. Where in the world did you hide this kind of talent?"

Paul was nodding. "This is phenomenal. It's the exact kind of uplifting hopefulness that people need. We've been talking about setting up socially distanced art showings, and virtual showings to get people back in the gallery. It's the creativity that people need right now. We need to stop simply existing and surviving and get back to the joy and happiness of being alive. How in the world did you come up with something so hopeful?"

I smiled and told them about the butterflies on the masks of the little girls in the store, that had seemed to take flight in front of me at one of the lowest points I had ever hit in my life. "It was those butterflies that brought color back to me. I realize now that I was horribly depressed from losing my sister, probably still am, but the discovery that color still exists in the world means that I can find a way to celebrate her without just mourning her through every breath I take."

Mona crossed the room and hugged me. As much as I knew we shouldn't be hugging, it was my exact need now. I leaned into her arms and felt the warmth of her hug and her caring to penetrate the outer shell of grayness that still existed around me, feeling it pop like a soap bubble in the air, and letting in all the color around me again. I didn't want to let her go, and just as I started to feel like I would need to, I felt Paul's arms around both of us and sank back into the hug. The human connection that had been missing from my life since Elsie had died was starting to feel like it was coming back.

The hug ended slowly, the three of us wrapped around each other surrounded by my paintings of butterflies taking flight.

Paul was the one to break the silence. "We'd be honored if you'd let us use this series of paintings in our opening. Can we see your other work?" I nodded, somewhat overcome with emotion. *They liked it! They really liked it!*

I showed them canvas after canvas, as we laughed and cried and reminisced over the paintings I had created with Elsie's encouragement. They loved all my work, but we all agreed that the newest paintings were by far the best I'd ever done.

"What are you naming your butterfly series?" Paul asked.

"*Elsie.*" They nodded and agreed that it was perfect.

Mona asked, "Was there anything Elsie was working on when she died?"

I nodded. "She told me she was working on a sculpture in her room. She had quarantined in there when she tested positive but made sure to take clay in with her to work on something small. When I took her to the hospital, she didn't say if she had finished it. I haven't been able to bring myself to go in and look."

They headed for her room, and I let them. I wasn't ready to go in yet, but they were old friends, and had seen Elsie's room before, coming over for dinner parties and seeing art that she'd hidden in there away from dinner guests prior to a show. "Oh, my," I heard, Paul's voice. Mona gasped.

"What is it?" I asked, curiosity bringing me closer to the doorway that I'd been since helping her out of the room.

They opened the door.

Sitting on Elsie's desk was a clay sculpture in Elsie's classic style, one she had carved and molded and shaped herself. There were four butterflies rising on a cloud, each painted in successive colors of pink, purple and blue, with one escaping the rising cloud and heading off alone.

I was shocked. How had she known? "We have to display this with the paintings," I said. "It's her final goodbye. She's the butterfly escaping the cloud and heading off into the unknown."

They nodded. "We would have it no other way," Paul added, in a soft voice, as Mona squeezed my hand in support.

Three weeks later, I stood in a corner, wearing a mask, and overcome with emotion. I'd sold multiple paintings, and had several offers for *Elsie*, the whole series, as well as the sculpture, and had stood strong. They weren't for sale at any price.

I was planning to display them in our studio, to remind myself that art had brought me back to myself, that Elsie's art had sealed the deal. I'd visited the doctor to make sure that I wouldn't slip back into the grayness again, and the prescription was helping me to keep from losing the colors of life that made up my art and my soul. I never wanted to lose that again, my connection to art, to my sister, and to life.

Addie J. King is an attorney by day and author by nights, evenings, weekends, and whenever else she can find a spare moment. Her novels, *The Grimm Legacy, The Andersen Ancestry, The Wonderland Woes, The Bunyon Barter,* and *The Perrault Vow* are now available from Hydra Publications. Her novel, *Shades of Gray,* is the first book in *The Hochenwalt Files* series and is also available. A collection of her short stories has been published, entitled *Demons, Heroes, and Robots, Oh My!* and is available exclusively on Amazon. Her website is addiejking.com

The New Pointillist Manifesto

Carlos Hernandez

1.

THE POINT was to give every last person on Earth the power to shape reality.

That was how the advertising copy read, anyway, the press releases from Chimp2Data, the speeches from the government officials on the take who signed off on it.

"From thin air," said musician / producer / scandalmaestro Roach Clip, in the most famous commercial for NaNarnia, leveraging every last tooth in their chromatoplate smile, "everyone will be able to shape objects out of nothing, tap into the cloud and its wealth of information, work anywhere in the world, and join the largest entertainment platform humanity has ever known: 24/7, all for free. Welcome to the future: where reality is only limited by the power of your imagination."

No one believed Roach Clip, of course—just another celeb grabbing their bag at 14:59. Yet, somehow, 400 million people had heard enough about NaNarnia to sign up for it in the first month. Two years later, NaNarnia had nearly five billion users worldwide.

Five years after that, the United Nations passed a resolution declaring access to NaNarnia a human right. The ability to control the countless nanites floating in the air around you, allowing you to shape them into tools that would last about as long as a workday (so long as your NaNarnia account was in good standing); access the universal library of human knowledge known as Web 6.0; monitor the recondite workings of your organs as easily as daydreaming; bid for jobs anywhere on the planet (very important, since all jobs had gone freelance); widen the scope and breadth of your senses until you found yourself looking down on Earth from 35,000 feet and could see for yourself how tiny and insignificant you were, thereby putting your hopes and dreams into geographically-swallowed relief.

All these features were declared by the U.N., by unanimous vote, essential to the modern human condition. Your human dignity was being insulted if you, too, could not sign up for a free account with NaNarnia. Everyone should be able to exercise control over reality via the nanotechnological medium that was now as ubiquitous as air. The world, after so many generations of useless fantasizing, was really and truly magical now. Now, we were all wizards.

Fifteen years after NaNarnia ended its long, long beta, having an account became opt-out only, in every country in the world. Ever after, every first breath that every baby in the world took was laden with so many Chimp2Data nanites, the number might as well have been infinite.

2.

The point, of course, was not to give every last one of the 18.6 billion persons on Earth the power to shape reality.

Reality must be agreed-upon, after all, lest the world collapse in a cataclysm of 18.6 billion competing hottakes. There must needs be a hierarchy. Some people shouldn't have some information. Some people needed to have the ability to override, overwrite, undo what others did. Some people's searches needed to be blocked, and their accounts flagged for having searched certain search terms. Some people needed the power to disempower those who needed disempowering.

Wealth decided—wealth has always decided—the distribution of power. NaNarnia was free to access and use, sure: but thousands of tiers of premium accounts, add-on abilities, features, skins, macros, licenses, and signature services granted special privileges to those who could afford them. Some police officers, for instance, had the ability to manifest firearms out of thin air, ranging from a simple Glock to a 22 K Hornet rifle, with a muzzle velocity of 2445 ft/s and an effective range of 240 yards—but only if their precincts could afford the "Law Enforcement Deluxe" tier. Most units had to settle for less expensive packages, as the Law Enforcement Deluxe tier ran 541 CNY per officer, per month.

Officers could upgrade themselves individually to a Law Enforcement Deluxe package, and often did, via crowdfunding campaigns. And since supporting a nanopowerful cop carried all sorts of advantages for anyone who expected a higher-than-average level of interaction with law enforcement, crowdfunding officers were seldom short on backers.

But you didn't have to be in law enforcement to enjoy all the deadly benefits of the Law Enforcement Deluxe package; any rich private citizen could upgrade themselves, as long as the local government allowed it. And generally speaking, governments did. It was better for freedom, and for the taxes they collected from NaNarnia, to punish offenders after the fact than to prevent preventable tragedies.

3.

The point, really, was to give everyone the illusion of power.

In a series of leaked documents—which unambiguously exposed the absolute corruption of Chimp2Data executives, and which had absolutely no consequences for either said executives nor the company—the world learned of "The Hotspur Strategy" of building a resilient, ever-growing, ever-profitable user-base.

Hotspur, you'll remember from your Shakespeare, is brash, opinionated, hot-headed, not a bad guy, but not nearly as good as he thinks he is, either as a fighter or a lover, and positively useless as a thinker. He's—spoiler!—a dead man by the end of the play, a victim of his own miscalculations and overestimations. Prince Hal says some nice things over his corpse:

> *"When [Hotspur's] body did contain a spirit,*
> *A kingdom for it was too small a bound..."*

According to the leaked docs, Chimp2Data execs saw themselves as noble Prince Hals and the rest of humanity as a legion of headstrong Hotspurs. Let them mouth off, cast insults, win useless victories of wit on social media, often against bots who were specifically designed to get dunked on by you and make you feel good about yourself.

Let them complain and threaten, said the execs; let them protest and plot. Give them the illusion they have control of their destiny. Use freedom of expression as a loss-leader.

Chimp2Data did not need to slay their Hotspurs in single combat. Single combat was for suckers. Hotspur, you see, valued principles over money. That was his true fatal flaw, the one that would keep him forever disempowered. Prince Hal would have done much better to drain Hotspur's coffers and max out his credit cards, keep him forever in debt.

This is the lesson of dragons: for all their physical prowess, their real power lay in the hoards they slept on.

That is why, in NaNarnia, you can know, free of charge, that the pain in your left side is indeed cancerous. You can learn exactly what type of cancer, what the prognosis is, how it might be treated had one the wherewithal, and more or less how long you had to live if you did not have the wherewithal, all without paying a cent. You would also learn—you had to learn, the targeted advertising that knew you had cancer wouldn't not let you learn—that there might be ways to use NaNarnia's nanotechnology to cure your cancer. Your visual and audio overlays would become a cataract of cancer ads inundating your virtual existence: which is to say, your entire existence, for when were you not logged into NaNarnia? You had no choice but to know that all of NaNarnia's life-saving technology could be yours for a mere 2,199 CNY a month.

The 17.9 billion people on Earth who could not afford 2,199 CNY a month for nanotechnological interventions would have to take their chances with whatever medicines they could afford, relying on whatever imperfect treatment they trusted most. But whether or not they could do anything about it, they would know how the disease progressed, daily, hourly, moment to moment.

With NaNarnia, you knew so much about everything and could do very little about anything. And whatever vitiated effect you could have on the world could be overridden in an instant by an overeager community standards bot who would time you out of NaNarnia—from work, school, entertainment, access to knowledge, access to your own body, life—for an algorithmically generated period of time that the algorithmically controlled community standards bot determined was fair: or you paid the fine. Whatever effort you took to influence the world was, by design, impermanent, mutable, instantly delible, and most definitely recorded and noted as part of your user profile, which was more importantly you than the ego you carried in your meat.

Or it was. Until the New Pointillists offered another way.

4.

A side point that turns out to be the entire point: humanity has always used technologies before it understood the consequences of them.

Take, for instance, quantum storage. Every nanite is an invisible floating qubit, holding information in a possibility space of outcomes yet to be determined. Nanites network with each other, both locally and across space and time, expanding the repertoire of what might be, theoretical outcomes multiplying ad infinitum, a cosmos of what-ifs added after every tick of the clock. All of this knowledge, all of this potential, entangled and pre-conceptualized, just waiting for a mind—an opinionated, desirous, Hotspur-raging mind—to step in and transform a superpositional notion into a dream come true.

Chimp2Data thought they could limit access to this qubitical Wonderland through money. But money is a construct. A construct is information. And information is the multiverse's ultimate currency.

Unlike quotidian currencies, however, information does not rely on a principle of scarcity. Quite the opposite: information is the only weapon against entropy. The purpose of information is to create more information, as that is the only way to forestall a multiversal end to everything.

NaNarnia made it possible for individual minds to access Information through a frame that, those cartoonish, was preferable to ontological truth: virtual reality. It further created, via nanites, a perfect bridge between the virtual and the bodily. Now the difference between a thought and a reality, a vision and an ontological truth, was limited only by the materials at hand. (Plus Newtonian laws. And quantum interactions.)

And, for a short time in human history, filthy lucre. With breathtaking hubris, NaNarnia tried to use puny human money to control what is literally the currency of all existence: capital-I Information. It failed.

Well, it will fail. Thanks to us, the New Pointillists. And with your help.

5.

Georges Pierre Seurat (1859-1891) is widely regarded as the world's premiere practitioner of that style of art historians term Pointillism. His world-famous *A Sunday Afternoon on the Island of La Grande Jatte* kicked off the Neo-Impressionism movement and ushered in a new understanding of how the eye makes sense of color, contrast, shape, texture, and light.

We members of the New Pointillists revere Seurat as the Saint of Synecdoche, Master of the Metonym, the God of the Gestalt. From him, we learned the infinite value of a point.

A point, mathematically speaking, has no length or width or height. It is a coordinate non-space that has no real-world corollary. When, in Geometry class, we draw a punctus on a Cartesian plane, we are always, by definition, drawing it infinitely too large. It's a useful way to help us visualize what is conceptually happening, but it's at best a model. At worst, it is an illusion.

But geometry is to quantum mechanics as an eyeball is to eyesight. The error that proved fatal to Chimp2Data's dreams of world domination is that they took their definition of a point from mathematics rather than art.

As we learn from Seurat, a point very much exists: it has mass and is perceptible as a speck of color on a canvas. Color, we learn from Seurat, is mutable, unstable, a shifting, scintillating thing. Color depends on what other colors are near it. That means any color is more than one color. Every dot in a work of Pointillism is also all the dots in its proximity, square-dancing riotously together, fueled by moonshine and a wild, demonic fiddle.

A Pointillist dot is a qubit. And qubits hold untold possibilities.

In a great work of Pointillism, every dot becomes the entire painting, because there is no extracting a dot from its dance with the other dots that have, together, created the unified image before you. A work of Pointillism is always a million works of Pointillism all at once, an explosion of paintings hurtling toward the eye, fusillading you with the immensity of what it is to have a thinking mind that can organize seemingly random radiation into knowable nouns.

You are a work of Pointillism. This is not a metaphor. Your points are not oils on canvas; yours are nanites. Those nanites have been governing your reality, rewriting your body, assigning you a societal value based on proprietary algorithms that are protected under the law as trade secrets. Most importantly, they have limited your agency in the world, dictating the limits of your creations.

But even as they were describing your limits, you were filling them with the infinite possibilities of your imagination. You imparted to them your preferences and predilections, your tastes, your rules, your shortcuts and life-hacks, your means of getting through the day. The nanites within you were slowly soaked through by your soul. And now that your soul is in them, there's no getting it out, no matter how much Chimp2Data would like to. And whatever has your soul within it is yours.

All you have to do is decide that, henceforth, you will govern all that would presume to house your soul.

6.

New Pointillism, like any art, requires tremendous rigor.

You have made it here, to this manifesto. You found us. That means that you already have what it takes. You are centered enough, uncontrollably imaginative, fuming like Hotspur on the field of battle.

The rest is practice.

Do not start small. Too many teachers tell students to start small. But all art is the expression of the soul, and the soul is bigger than anything that can exist through the vehicle of matter.

So start big. Attempt, with all earnestness and all the force of your will, to make yourself into a god.

Whatever a god means to you, be it: lightning from fingertips, sudden tempests, augury of the future, resurrection of the dead.

Fellow New Pointillist, you will fail. Of course you will fail: art requires rigor. From failure, your godliness will grow. You will learn the intricacies of nanites, your new medium.

Nanites, you will find, are as willful and wanton as minnows in a lake. Do not try to govern the minnows. Be the lake. The minnows will react to their environment. Govern them not through fiat nor force. You are their world. Change the environment within they wander, and they will adapt and become what is required to flourish in that environment.

There will never be a time when your medium will always obey you. Would you want it to? Nanites are quantum; they are strange and charmed and, taken together, spooky. Because they are haunted, they can be haunted. It is the job of every artist to haunt their medium. You, new New Pointillist, must haunt the nanites that haunt you.

With practice, NaNarnia's tier levels will become less of a barrier to you. Soon, you will pay less and less for access, and then, one day, nothing. Meanwhile, your command over the n-ocean will rival increasing levels of authority. There are New Pointillists who have the clearance of presidents, even though they have been cleared by no one, save themselves. They have saved themselves.

Make good art, New Pointillist. Art is good when it expands infinity. Greed adores scarcity; good art attacks greed. Use your art to deprescribe the possible. We cannot wait to see the mark you will leave on reality's canvas.

And don't forget to sign your work. Pseudonymously—we don't want you to get caught—but sign it. History needs to know who to thank.

⌐——

New York Times Bestselling author **Carlos Hernandez** is the author of *The Assimilated Cuban's Guide to Quantum Santeria, Sal and Gabi Break the Universe* (which won the Pura Belpré award in 2019) and *Sal and Gabi Fix the Universe*, along with many short stories, poems, and works of drama. By day, Carlos is a CUNY Professor of English and a game designer: most recently, Negocios Infernales, the TTRPG he is co-creating with C. S. E. Cooney. Find him on socials @writeteachplay

A Matter of Value

Daniel Myers

I GREW UP ON THE WARNINGS. My father always said, "Anyone who lets themselves get scammed has only themselves to blame." The family motto, right along with, "Do unto others."

I suppose I should explain. I mean, there's probably someone out there who hasn't read about the Roffe kid who got taken to the cleaners.

In my defense, I suppose, while I've struggled to understand the rules of games, I live for their art.

—

You see, back at Ballard prep school I'd seen a magazine article about an artist who was making weird chess sets. They were intended to explore the history of the game and highlight all the variations of board and pieces. I'd played chess, of course. Everyone there did. There were regular practices and tournaments, and even special classes, though no matter how hard I tried, I was never good enough to bother with them.

But the chess boards in that article were different. They had too many squares or too few. The shapes were wrong, triangles and diamonds and hexagons instead of squares. There was even a board painted on the outside of a globe. I bought the few that I could find and tried them with whoever I could get to play, but I still kept losing. And they lost their appeal.

I gave up and found more productive interests. I graduated, went to college, graduated again, took over the reins of one of the family companies, and made my parents happy by being boring and making money.

Until about two years ago at an upstate gallery when I saw the McCall-White chess set. And the very unfortunate moment when I met Liz Cooper.

—

"It's marked 'Not For Sale' but I can get it for you."

It took a moment before I realized the words were directed towards me. I half-turned towards the speaker. "Excuse me?"

"The chess set. If you're interested in buying it, I know the artist and can arrange the sale."

"No, I'm not interested, thank you."

She snorted derisively—honest-to-God full up snorted—like the lie was that obvious. Really? I actually pulled my eyes away from the display to get a look.

If you've never seen Liz before, she's the sort of person described as "non-descript". I mean, if she were really tall, or red-headed, or a bodybuilder, I could give you a way to spot her in a crowd. Liz is . . . none of those. She's also not strikingly beautiful, or notably dressed. The best I can come up with is that if you imagine the sort of person who works, unnoticed, in the background to make sure everything is going smoothly, she looked exactly like what you're thinking. You know, the perfect executive assistant.

I put on my best swagger. "What makes you think I want to buy it?"

"You're in a gallery wearing an expensive but conservative suit. So you're not an artist. You didn't come in with anyone and don't seem to be looking for anyone, so you're not someone's guest. Right so far?"

Hmm. "Yes. I suppose I do look the part. But why this piece?"

She snorted again. I squinted.

"That's just plain observation," she deadpanned. "You never look at price tags and ignore any artwork that's even remotely challenging. But you've stood *here* for the past twenty minutes, and have looked for the price twice." She then smiled in a way that was somehow irritating and friendly at the same time.

I took the business card she offered, mostly hoping it'd make her leave, and as she walked away I got the distinct feeling she was always on the winning side.

The winning side, I repeated to myself. Of what?

———

You already know I called her. And bought the chess board. The moment she'd said she could get it there really was no other possible outcome. I simply had to have it.

The board was circular, which was uncommon enough, and the spaces were segmented out in fine silver lines over a black starfield. The light and dark gray pieces were made to look like the ones from that medieval Scottish set, but with a sci-fi theme: space suits and ray guns. Each piece was unique, and what really got me—all of them wore expressions of puzzlement.

A month later she sent me pictures of a box of parts for a three-dimensional chess set that had been used on screen in an old sci-fi series. They needed cleaning and restoration, but even with that the price was a steal. I bought it.

More calls. A Japanese chess set that had belonged to the emperor, an original Frazetta painting used for the cover of "The Chessmen of Mars", one of Rubik's puzzle prototypes, card game proof sheets, first edition board games, posters from early game conventions, artwork for countless collectible card games, and the original hand-typed rules to dozens of role-playing games. The more obscure the items were, the more I wanted them. And then came the topper.

"Hi, Tad? It's Liz. Was just contacted by someone selling an entire collection of weird chess boards he made for an art project way back. They've been sitting in his attic for years but he says they're ok. Call me back if you want them."

I actually got to meet the guy. Nice guy. He was in poor health, both physically and mentally, but he was cheerful. I'm sure I acted like a weirdo, but what the heck, he didn't care. I thanked him, handed him a check, and stayed in a happy daze the whole time while Liz drove me to the airport. "I'm on a later flight," she said, dropping me off at the terminal. "I've got to arrange for movers and a truck to get everything shipped back."

———

The artwork kept arriving, and I started to feel alarmed. Yes, each piece was being checked over for cleaning and conservation issues before they were shipped to me, but I hadn't really realized just how many pieces I was buying. My flat in Borough Park was going to be packed full of crates by the end of the month. So I took the obvious solution; I opened a museum.

The place was only a couple of miles away. It was an old Lutheran church and school that had been closed down and auctioned off. Because of the big housing slump the new owner was in a tight spot, so we both made out pretty well in the deal. I hired a bunch of guys to clean it up and upgrade the security systems. Then I had all the art moved over there and locked up in the classrooms upstairs while the rest of the place was renovated.

I honestly thought it was all going great. I mean it's not like I spent the money on coke and strippers. This was art! And a solid investment, right? Besides, there had to be some kind of tax deduction from the museum, and I had to store the art somewhere.

———

I've been thinking about it a lot over the past few months, and I'm pretty sure the first hint of doubt crept in at the museum's opening day. The old sanctuary was the only room that was ready, and the public opening was still months away, but Eddie, my accountant, had been begging for a little positive cash flow from "that art thing." So I picked out some of the biggest and prettiest works to put on display, hired some caterers, and invited a bunch of . . .

Ok, I was going to say "friends" but that's not it. These were people I knew from business dealings, from back at school, and a bunch with similar connections to my parents. My only real interest in them is that they were the sort of people who would pay to be "Friends of the Museum." They'd get their names on a plaque in the lobby, and I'd get Eddie to shut up for a bit.

Liz had invited some game artists along with a couple of writers I'd never heard of; I suppose to the guests they were almost as interesting as the artwork. That was her mistake.

I did my part - easy because it's the sort of thing my parents had diligently trained me for. I put on my best and most believable fake smile and schmoozed like a suit salesman. In a way it was kind of fun, and I'm pretty good at it after all, but after hearing—or even saying—the same fake line for the dozenth time it began to wear thin.

That's when I recognized this artist who had just walked in. I'd met him at the big convention in Atlanta earlier that year. To be completely honest, I'd have been happy to hear stories from the city sewer inspector if it got me away from my mom's old college roommate, but I actually wanted to talk with this guy. I made a patently insincere apology to Marge (sorry, mom) and headed in his direction.

"Mr. Asplund! I'm so glad you could make it."

He looked and paused for a fraction of a second and broke into a friendly smile.

"Mr. Roffe! It's good to see you again. Please, call me Randy."

"So what do you think?" I gestured toward the exhibits. "I don't think there's a bigger collection of games and game art anywhere. At least not on display."

He glanced around the room and nodded appreciatively. "It's very impressive. I've heard you've only been collecting for a year, but this is a wonderful start." His response seemed completely sincere. Maybe it really was.

"It's more than a start," I offered. "As soon as the rest of the work is finished it will have over fifteen thousand square feet of gallery space, and the art is ready and waiting to fill it all up. We're even going to have a whole room of card game art; that's where your painting will be featured." I couldn't help but grin as I waited for him to work through all that. It was perfect. The only improvement would have been if he had a drink, because I know he'd have sprayed it. Yes, I pictured it.

"You've got one of mine here?"

"Of course," I said, and pointed to the far back corner, right behind the pulpit. "It's the one of the bishop's miter." I'd been proud of that placement.

At this point I'll admit that I'm much more used to being around accountants than artists, so his reaction kind of threw me off. He spotted the painting and scowled at it, about the same way I might if someone redecorated my apartment while I was at lunch. Without another word he crossed the room, weaving around the well-dressed chatting groups of walking money, and I followed in his wake with an unfamiliar feeling growing in the pit of my stomach.

He barely glanced at the painting, but moved to read the label on the wall next to it. I heard him make a faint "huh" sound, and then he looked back at the art.

"Is . . . is something wrong?" I asked.

He looked at me and visibly relaxed. "No, no. I was just caught off guard. The label . . ." He paused and restarted, "I'm really surprised they would have sold it." He looked back at the painting and almost scowled at it again.

"Do you think it's a fake? I've got a friend who wound up with a forged Dali."

"What? Oh, no. It's my work. I intentionally painted this one using as close to accurate medieval materials and style as possible. See how this is mounted beneath the glass? And how that corner has a slight curl to it?"

I looked where he was pointing, but honestly I had no clue. I'd bought it because it was interesting. In spite of the large frame, the painting was only about seven inches across. The work itself though was incredibly detailed. The background was all scrolling leaves and ribbons in bright green, red, and blue. And in the foreground was a miter with accents in gold leaf.

He explained how to tell parchment from pergamenata, how the gold was applied, and how he ground very specific minerals to make his own paints.

"So it really is the original art?" I'd thought it was, but he'd made me so nervous.

He waved a dismissive hand. "Yes. I remember painting it very well. There is absolutely no doubt that it's my work," he said, and then he quietly added to himself, "Why would they have decided to sell it?"

———

Good enough, right? I mean, Asplund did confirm the painting as being his. But it woke up the little beast of mistrust that my parents had so carefully cultivated in me. I started to question first the rationality, and then the actual possibility of amassing an art collection like I had in only 18 months. Normally I would take any art questions I had to Liz, but if there was something off about all of this she would be at the center. So I started to look into things on my own . . . and immediately ran into a roadblock.

I had almost never been in contact with any of Liz's sources. I had no phone numbers, no anything. Sometimes I had a name because I'd written a check, but even then it was usually for a broker or holding company. I didn't mind, as it kept my hands clean of any possible legal issues; that was how my dad had always run things. Liz had told me it kept me mysterious and she could get better deals that way.

The couple of contacts I did have were instant dead-ends. The artist from the article? He'd been moved to a care facility shortly afterwards, and had died the following month. The importer of the emperor's chess set refused to speak to me. The place that sold me the Frazetta took my call, but said there wasn't anything to tell me beyond what was on the paperwork that came with the painting. I looked at that paperwork again and everything was as straightforward as could be. Really no more than a glorified receipt, which felt a bit disappointing for a painting that cost me just over a million.

The next time Liz called me with a lead—a prop game board used in some 1990's kids movie—I asked, prepped to stand my ground, to meet the seller. I don't know what I expected, but it certainly wasn't, "Sure, no problem. They're in LA. Do you want it to be face-to-face or video?" When I said "in person" she told me she'd schedule it and call back. She didn't. That was on Friday, and on Monday morning I got a call from my accountant.

"Sorry to bother you so early, Tad," Eddie said. "I got an odd letter last week for your museum from someone who wants the painting they loaned back. You should have told me some of those were on loan. It brings the exposure down a bit, but if the total value is significant enough we might need to report it to investors."

"Wait, no," I sputtered out. "That's not right. Everything in that museum is owned outright. There's not even a lien on the building."

"Which I told you was a bad idea from a tax viewpoint, but you insisted. Anyway, need to clear this up. Have Liz send me a copy of the bill of sale, along with whatever other paperwork she has. I don't want any more surprises until *after* tax time."

Liz wasn't answering her phone.

By the time I thought to call the bank and close the accounts we'd set up to cover things like small purchases and agent fees, it was too late. It wasn't a huge amount, but a couple of hundred thousand isn't exactly pocket change either.

I took a walk to the museum, unlocked the front door, and went in. You wouldn't believe how hard it was to not look at the sign that said, "Opening Soon!" I could feel it staring at me as I walked past. I hadn't realized before that signs could be so scornful.

I walked back to the painting of the miter, and I realized it was really beautiful. The label said it was the only card in the game illustrated with medieval techniques. A 15th century Italian style, painted on goat parchment. The pigments were hand-ground, and included genuine vermilion, lapis lazuli, and malachite. I gazed at it in wonder as well as confusion. It looked real enough. The artist himself said it was real. But something sure as hell had bothered him about it.

It's hard for me to confess, that's when it occurred to me to actually look the thing up. I got out my phone and did a search, and there at the top was a picture of the painting, and right after that was another one that was slightly different.

The original artwork that had actually been used in the game was painted on illustration board. It was very similar but the colors weren't quite the same, and it had yellow paint instead of gold leaf. So while the painting I was looking at wasn't the original for the game, it still was an original painting of the same theme by the same artist. It was also, at least in my opinion, the nicer of the two. According to internet fan sites, this "revised" painting was made as a private commission, and the owner was thrilled with how it had turned out. There was no price listed and no word anywhere of it being sold, let alone to me.

What had I done? I stared at it a bit longer, and thought about how the colors and shapes just made me feel . . . happy, and that the real owner probably felt that way too.

Then my phone rang.

"How screwed am I, Liz?" It wasn't the most conventional greeting, but it efficiently got the conversation moving in the right direction.

"Oh, you'll never know the full extent of what I've done."

She said it coldly, but with a hint of amused chuckle, or maybe gloating. Either way, I didn't like it. I understand games; I grew up running from them. But when you've beaten someone you should have the courtesy to be gracious about it. No, wait, more than that—I'd never agreed to play.

"Really?" I snapped. "I can have appraisers and auditors go over everything and have a detailed report in my hands within a week. It'd be expensive but that's one answer I know I'll get."

"That's not what I meant, Tad, and you know it. This isn't about money. What you don't realize is just how badly I've cursed you."

Ok, I'll admit that part surprised me.

"Cursed?"

"Yes. Very much so. And I'm not going to tell you whether it's a real curse or just metaphorical—it doesn't matter. You're cursed."

I tried to respond, to say something sharp, and at least slightly mean, but it took too long for me to work through what she was saying. The best I could do was let out a sort of quiet "unh" sound. She must have heard it as, "how," or maybe she didn't care. She just kept talking.

"There is at least one object in your collection that is an outright forgery, but it's probably not the one you'd expect. There are many which have values that are very close to or even greater than what you paid. The thing is that one of those very real objects has the curse, and for as long as you own it the curse will affect you."

"Your collection will have a value for as long as you believe it has value. As your certainty falters, so will that value. If you get everything appraised out of uncertainty your collection will become completely worthless, along with everything else in your life. On the other hand, if you never sell any of it and keep people from looking too closely it will keep its value . . . but you won't actually have the money." Halfway through that last sentence she actually laughed. Then, I realized. I'd never heard her laugh.

"Oh, one more thing," she continued, "If you try really hard you might be able to find me, but I'll also start talking about what's real and what isn't, and the curse will take its toll. Do you understand now?"

I did, and I didn't like it. I still had one question though.

"Why? What the hell did I ever do to you?"

"My God, you are as much of a dolt now as you were back at Ballard! You really don't remember me at all?"

"At Ballard?"

"You and your friends taught me a valuable lesson about playing games; whenever you find you can't win, flip the table so your opponent can't either."

Vague, uncomfortable memories of chess games materialized, and being sneered at for always losing. I saw the board knocked off the table, more than once, but one of those might have involved a mean but otherwise forgettable girl.

I may have made some sound as it all came back to me, but I can't be sure.

"So you *do* remember! Good," she sneered. "You were ahead in the game. There was no way I could ever catch up to the position you had at the start, so I flipped the table. Go ahead and pick up the pieces. Maybe even ask someone else to play. Just be aware that we two aren't the only ones playing." She snorted.

I hung up the phone, and deleted her number.

Daniel Myers is a database programmer, author, inept raconteur, and food historian. This means his writings often involve food, which can be a bit unusual if they're database extracts or horror stories. He lives in Ohio with his family and an impressive number of Figgy-Fizz bottle caps. Currently he runs MedievalCookery.com, which is where he puts his research notes and recipes from medieval France and England.

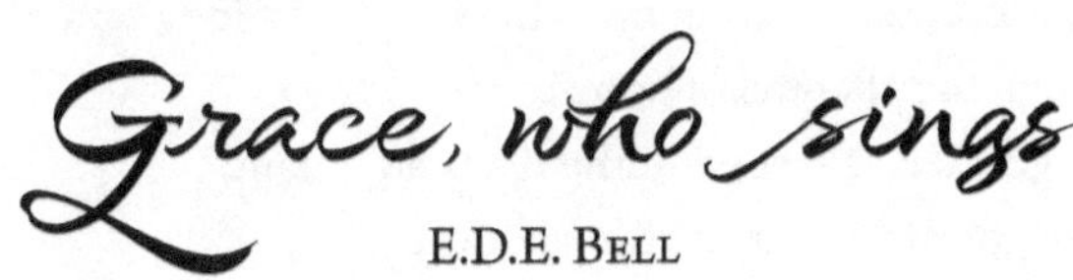

Grace, who sings

E.D.E. Bell

GRACE KNELT at the next bedside. Easing the cover away, e found the soldier's twitching hand and held it.

Pain coursed through em. Deep pain, but Grace could not heal it all, not and keep energy for the next bed. A wound. Shards of metal. Enchanted metal, meant to bury. The pain, so sharp. E'd have to hurry to prevent passing out like the soldier before em.

Pulling in a wavering breath, e sang. Not in words; words were forbidden. There was no pain to justify words, e knew. And so Grace drew from sound. Low notes, melancholy, pulling and lifting away the metal, the damage, coaxing cells of skin together. Another piece, deeper. Eir voice dropped, the notes guttural in both exhaustion and need. The metal fell away, rough shards now caught against the side of the soldier's gown.

E let go. Falling back into a seat, the pain rushed back into its unwitting host as Grace grasped deep breaths.

Conserving strength, or sometimes the illusion of it, e crawled across the spotless floor, eir layered linen pants worn but suited for such things, and reached for the next bed, pulling emself up to sit as eir eyes crossed the slate on which was chalked, "Fawna, she".

"Hello," the soldier said through darting eyes, rising suddenly to sit. "Thank Mercy." She reached out her hand.

Another wave. A broken ankle stabbed with flashes of warmth while alarms of trauma clanged like broken bells, so discordant e could barely focus on the ankle through them. No resources to heal all, and a soldier needed to move. Eyes closing at the discomfort of Fawna's unsettled gaze, Grace lilted in mid-tones, letting a long note thread and catch through the channel of bones.

E let go. "Ice," e rasped to the tent's attendant.

"She's good?" The man stepped over.

"Ice," Grace repeated. "She can't go back out until the swelling subsides."

Grace crawled again, to the next, ignoring the growing murmurs. Four more for now, and it helped no one to wait.

Cord sat steady on the bed, the covers bunched underneath him. "Just a gash," he said. "Skip me; save your energy."

"Could get infected," Grace murmured, reaching for his hand. He placed the other atop eirs, the warmth a momentary comfort.

Grief. Anger. Resolve. There it was, across his upper arm. Into the muscle. E hummed, rising into a low wail, and the edges knit into place. E sat back, willing eir eyes not to stay closed for too long, lest they find the sleep within them.

"I'm good." Cord preempted the attendant's query, and rose from the bed. "What about em?" Cord pointed eir way.

"We all do our duty," the attendant answered, a cube of ice bouncing between his palms. He moved along. As did Grace.

A thin figure lay atop the sheet. Eyes calm, strong arm muscles twitching. "Threw my back," they whispered. "No one even hit me."

If Grace had strength, e could try and adjust the soldier's skeleton, but only the magic held em from collapse emself. How many beds? Two more. Then a rest. Rhythm, this would take. E held the soldier's hand, letting eir own body sway into a beat, guiding finely tuned notes to find each segment and joint, to ease the tension that held them.

Grace cried out. In eir exhaustion, e'd almost fallen. Just as physically, one could walk into a lightly covered hole, what e'd found was a deep pit. E struggled, holding the song as e teetered on its edge. The depth of this sadness was not a thing to be healed. Only, it could be bridged.

"Tell me," Grace pled. "Or I cannot reach you." Not easily. Not with the strength e had. Not with two more waiting.

"It's a lie," they whispered, so quietly Grace wasn't sure if e heard it, or felt it through the bond. "Our mission. A lie. Laced with truths, like poisoned candy."

Images flashed before them. A kindly man. His face contorted as he screamed. A woman, behind him, pulling them aside. The ceiling of shelters, in the dark, watching each bump in the canvas as the rain fell upon it. "You'll need your rest!"

Another day. The sunlight and the glare. Arrows. Swords. A charge of forces, their emblems on caps. A howl from their side, and a body, slumped into snow. An elder, blurry, with head hung.

E was losing grip. Pushing each note like a hunted bird's cry, Grace snapped the bones into place, freeing them. Tension fell, and Grace let go.

"Two more," a thin voice called. Glaring light burst through the flap, as two litters pushed through and hasty hands above the mud-stained boots lifted the bodies onto freshly turned beds. E glanced back at the soldier; they were being helped to their feet.

Four, then, four more beds.

This one, sleeping. Fitfully. Grace pulled the sheet to reach for her hand. Wounds. Bruising. There, a hard break, in the leg. E sung low, and stopped. *No.* There was no time for this. Not the static or interruptions. *Quiet,* e hissed to emself. E sang again, low. Worried, for it would be worse to heal such a fracture poorly. E tried again, reaching into a song of depth, swaying eir body back and forth, much longer than it should have taken, but relieved, distantly, as the bone pushed into place. Then more, raising the tone as eir voice strained, and then cracked. But Grace did not get all the wounds, not enough. Perhaps e should try again. A moment, then. To clear.

"One more," the voice said.

Grace sat back.

"What is it?" The attendant, beside em.

E looked up, only now realizing e was leaning against a crate. "Distractions."

He nodded in sympathy, and went to help with the arrival.

The images in eir mind, e could not clear them. Like an infection, they had spread. Through eir haze, instincts took em, and without realizing e had done so, e started to sing. Words. Words in low, slow, melody.

My heart, my heart, for what you've been through
For I have felt it all
And the lies, the doubts that creep inside you
I could not help at all
This world, this world we'll shape together
Together we pull through
I cannot save you from these failures
For I have made them too
Atone
Atone
Atone
We atone

The words echoed in silence like long bells, and only then did Grace remember where e was.

The silence broke. "Healer. Outside," the attendant barked. "We'll deal with you later. Bring in an off-shift," e vaguely heard as e stumbled outside and sunk against a tree.

No one followed em. Nor could e walk, not yet, not to get away. What had e done? Make another healer suffer, dragged from sleep or rest. Caused soldiers to lie in pain. And no one followed. No one joined em.

For nothing, then.

A strong pair of arms lifted em into the air and began to move away. A familiar energy. "Cord," e remembered. "Arm wound." His arms were strong, and warm. But he did not understand.

"There are more to be healed," e informed. "Without me, they'll suffer."

"Then be with them," he answered. "But not here. Here, you'll be marked as traitor. I heard you," he added. "Your song."

"Their song," e murmured, but he did not understand.

—

When e awoke, the strong arms still surrounded em. E jostled in familiar rhythm. They were walking.

"Your pain," was what he said. "I feel it."

E did not answer.

Step after step, they trudged on. E heard the gravel. The birds. The beating of a soldier's heart.

And then, a song. Or, a humming. Low, and unsettled, the hum continued, over the few notes it could find. There were spells like this, e recalled. Songs of need.

When the voice grew silent, Grace was not healed. But e was comforted. "I believe, now, that I can walk," e said.

Slowly, carefully, Cord set em down. Before them, Grace saw a village ahead. Uneasy and alone, e was grateful when his large hand met eirs.

"There is an inn," was all he said. "This way."

Cord's insignias had been cast aside, Grace noted. Yet he could not hide, not with the manner of a soldier, e worried. Surely, they would know.

As they walked together through the propped-open doors of the multi-story inn, it was not Cord who was noticed.

"A healer," someone gasped. "Look, the marks."

Grace glanced around, more alert now, as people moved toward em, hands raised.

"No," Cord said, stomping a bit harshly, but stopping their movements. "A person. E is a singer."

"I am hurt," someone said, pushing to the front. "Will e help me?"

"What have you done?" another chided. "When I have waited—"

An elder tapped a cane against the floor. "What does e sing?" As if demanding an answer.

Grace found emself answering. An unexpected answer. "Truths."

Cord's expression drew slightly. He accompanied Grace to a bench, sitting beside em as the people gathered, but not too close.

"Will you sing with me?" e asked him, watching the gruff face of the soldier, now traitor too.

"No," he said again. "But I will protect you as you do."

Grace laughed. Maybe some would not see the humor, but this type of humor had been all e had, to get through each day before. But there was more. More to it. Joy, e realized. E laughed for joy.

"Well, then," e said, feeling new energy. "A song. For you."

For this first song, there were no words. Cries. Every tone, every melody e had ever used, flowed through, and with them, the memories, some clear, some covered, of the soldiers e had met. For the words, forbidden.

The elder rose, and dropped a coin onto the table. "For a drink, if you'll do another."

Words, then. Were they ever forbidden . . . e considered with a start. Words.

Grace calmed emself. And sang.

> *It's a song about no one*
> *It's a song about you*
> *Who's here to join me in it*
> *And then, what will you do?*

> *Sing a song about friendship*
> *Sing a song as we yearn*
> *Sing a song about the pain we share and*
> *The hell we will burn*
> *Look, the smile on that watching face*
> *Look, the gleam in that eye*
> *Look, the frown on the one who will not*
> *And the meaning of why*
> *It's a song about no one*
> *It's a song about you*
> *You're here to join me in it*
> *Is that what you will do?*
> *Life.*
> *Our life.*
> *Praise life.*
> *Our life.*

Eir voice had steadied, drawn longer, with each line.

Grace thought e might go on, but e was tired, still. And the words trailed off. E scooped up the coin that had been placed on the table, and handed it to Cord. Around them, the patrons whispered and talked. No more coins were laid down. And Grace was tired. But, perhaps, was e free?

The weight was so heavy.

"Now what?" e asked Cord, feeling a new spirit, not yet well, but the idea of it settling.

Cord glanced around. "What do you want to do?"

Grace breathed.

E.D.E. Bell (she or e) loves fantasy fiction, and enjoys blending classic and modern elements. A passionate vegan and earnest progressive, Bell feels strongly about issues related to equality and compassion. Her works are quiet and queer, and often explore conceptions of identity, community, friendship, family, and connection. She lives in Ferndale, Michigan, where she writes stories and revels in garlic. She is honored to have edited this anthology, grateful to have breathed in its passion, and delighted that the cover image is, mostly coincidentally, from her favorite family game. You can follow Emily's adventures at edebell.com.

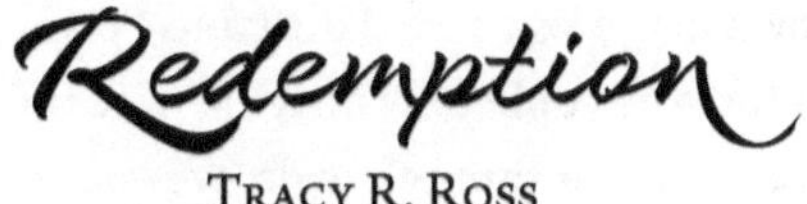

Redemption

Tracy R. Ross

Town of Rythixor—Realm of Kahrain

CommonYear 403

WITH A FINE LAYER OF SWEAT beading his brow, he walked down, down, down along the dark passageway. On either side was a dithihi from the Viper Elite of the Brotherhood of the Kronshue, both of whom would make certain that he went through Penance. His brethren had warned him that it was a little scary the first time, and more than a little painful, but he was nothing if not a man of his word. Regardless, he'd been paid handsomely for his work, and he felt the gold coins slipping and sliding past one another in his left pocket. It was an extraordinary feeling for someone who'd gone without for so many weeks and months of his life.

Ahead, he started to see a soft glow. It got bigger and brighter the further they went until finally they stood at the entry to an open door-way. Within the small, dimly-lit room was a young woman. She looked up from where she sat before a polished hinoki table, her eyes taking in the three dithihi. She made only the slightest of gestures with one hand and he was being thrust forward into the room and the door hastily shut behind him.

He just stood there for a moment, taking in the person before him. She was younger than he'd imagined, at least a couple years his junior. Her long, dark hair was twisted and bound by ornamental clips on each side above delicately shaped ears, only slender tresses from her temples softly cascading down to her shoulders. Her eyes were the color of the darkest chag, and as she looked at him, it almost seemed as though she was just as afraid of him as he was of her. But within a heartbeat, the impression was gone and she was confidently beckoning him closer.

He sat down in the seat across the table. Spread across the surface was a variety of tools he could only imagine were the staples of her profession. He gazed at them through wide eyes before the sound of her voice brought his attention back to her mesmerizingly beautiful face. "My name is Takarra. What is your name?"

His heart went out to her as he recalled what his brethren had told him a few days ago. "I . . . I'm sorry to hear about your mother. She was very respected within the Elite and will be greatly missed."

He felt a heat settle into his face before he turned away and inwardly admonished himself. The other dithihi had told him to be certain to give his condolences, and it had been the first thing to come out of his mouth. *Name, you fool. She asked for your name.*

"Th . . . thank you. That is very kind." At the tone in her voice, he looked up to see a shimmer of unshed tears. Takarra cleared her throat. "But I've been told this is your first Penance. You could never have met my mother."

He nodded. "That is true. But I am still sorry you lost her."

She slid her gaze back over to meet his. Once again, there was that moment of fear before it slipped away and was gone. "What is your name?"

"Artamaru."

She gave a small smile. "Alright, Artamaru. I'll get started." Her expression shifted to one of solemnity. "I need you to tell me some details of the one you killed and their name."

He was taken aback by her bluntness, but replied all the same. "What kind of details?"

She shrugged nonchalantly. "Just the reason why the person was targeted and the way they died."

He just stared at her for a moment. *Why would she want to know these things? The village women would never want to hear such things.*

But I guess she's not a typical village woman. "Don't you find that a bit morbid?"

She cocked her head. "I need to know so I can do my work."

He swallowed heavily, his fear returning. "What exactly are you going to do to me?"

She pierced him with eyes that suddenly seemed a bit more than what they had been when he first entered the little chamber. "You know the agreement. The Viper Elite does what it does, and in return for the gifts your brethren have undoubtedly disclosed, the Order of Farynaii takes reparations. It is the balance we have created."

He nodded and swallowed again. "He was Jailor Harantes. He was taking money in bribes."

Takarra frowned. "Doesn't almost everyone in any position of authority take bribes?"

Art returned the frown and his tone was gruff. "His kept rising."

She nodded and he could see her struggling to not crack a smile. After a moment of silence he realized she was waiting for more details. "I killed him with an ezekul blade across the throat."

She nodded again and singled out a couple of needle-like implements of different sizes. Both were made of sharpened bone with wooden handles, which she delicately placed before her on the table, followed by a series of vials filled with dark liquid.

Feeling as though she perhaps needed more, he continued. "It wasn't very difficult to do because he was asl—"

She raised a forestalling hand. "I think I have the information I need, thank you."

He nodded a bit contritely. *Details, but not too many details,* he thought and was quiet as she continued to prepare for her work. She got a small pot of heated water, laid out some clean cloths, opened the vials, and tested the tips of the pointed tools set before her. Finally, she held out a hand. "It is time. Please give me your arm."

"Wh . . . where are you going to put it?"

She was thoughtful. "Well, most prefer for their first ink to be displayed on the forearm where all can see, for it is a symbol of status and belonging. I was going to put it there." She pointed to a neutral place on his arm.

He shook his head. "No, I want it to be out of sight. I . . ." He hesitated as he hatched a reason why he didn't want to see the tattoos, something other than the reason that lay somewhere deep inside his soul. "I'd like to keep my profession hidden as long as possible. So, I'd prefer for it to be placed high on my chest near my shoulder."

She nodded, her expression speculative. "Of course. As you wish."

Takarra rose from her seat and approached him. "Please take off your shirt and move your chair sideways beside the table so that I may reach my tools and ink more easily."

He nodded and almost hesitantly moved to the place she'd indicated. He then removed the homespun shirt as she'd requested. Takarra took a cloth and poured some of the heated water over it. A scent wafted through the air, one that reminded him of lirylacs in spring. She then placed the cloth over his skin and he gave a swift inhale. It was much hotter than he thought it would be. She rubbed the cloth vigorously over his chest and shoulder as he took a look around the room. Strange runic images adorned the walls and ceiling and he wondered what they meant. She then removed the cloth and waited for the skin to cool down and dry. Meanwhile, she stood at his back, moving his jet-black, shoulder-length hair out of her way with deft fingers that hesitated on the nape of his neck, back, and shoulders. She began to whisper in a sing-song type voice, like an incantation to a spell.

All the while, the room seemed to darken. The wall sconces guttered.

Fear snaked through Artamaru's guts. "What is happening?"

"Shhh." She smoothed her fingertips over the prepared area. "It won't be long before I can start inking. Stay still. This won't hurt much."

And before he could utter a reply, her gentle breath blew across his flesh. It was something a lover might do, and it stirred his loins for a moment. Takarra quickly picked up one of her tools, dipped it into the ink, and pressed the tip into his skin.

Then the pain came.

It was a burning sensation, as though something was being branded there. He wanted to scream. He wanted to leap up from the chair and vacate the room to never return. Instead, he just clenched his teeth and squeezed his eyes tightly shut, wondering if it would feel this way every time.

Every time he killed someone.

———

CommonYear 411

Within the dim recesses of her room, Takarra picked up her mug and drank of the warm, deep brown contents. Chag was her favorite drink, and her mother's before her. She abruptly looked up from her book, sensing something just beyond her auditory perception. She was still for several moments, straining to hear before deciding it was nothing and going back to the words written on the pages, words written by the high priest of her order. She read the words every day, for they reminded her of her purpose in this life, and that through her service, she would one day be rewarded.

That thought bid her pause and her attention turned inward, away from the book. Memories of her training tumbled through her mind. Her mother had always used the utmost of patience with her young, wayward daughter, and that showed in the work Takarra did now. She was considered one of the best priestesses in the Order of Farynaii, and Viper Elite dithihi from all over the town of Rythixor came to her for Penance.

Magic. That's what Penance was. It was magic that liked to play a bit on the dark side.

And she was the vehicle, the Talent, through which it was expressed.

It was the existence she'd been raised for, one she was good at doing. But it was lonely, as her family line was the only one with the gift.

With that thought, her memories shifted to the first dithihi for whom she'd performed Penance. Without even knowing it, a small smile curved up one corner of her mouth. According to her mother, and her ancestors who had come before, it was the subject of this first Penance who was to be her destiny. She didn't truly understand it, but it was a phenomenon that had taken place for all ghigau down through the generations. Those for whom femininity drew their fates would be drawn to the ghigau, to the destiny it brought, and the one brought to them. Her own father had been a dithihi warrior who had been her mother's first.

Takarra tore herself away from that thought and focused her eyes back on the book. The lines of one of the verses leapt out at her, as always reminding her what she was: zhushexi ghigau—ink priestess of Farynaii.

And with her siren's voice,
The zhushexi ghigau shall call to the spirit of the deceased.
She shall call it and bind it to the dithihi,
Inking the spirit onto his flesh and thus into his soul.

The torchlight fluttered with an errant breeze that somehow made it this far beneath ground and Takarra looked up from the book, once again sensing a disturbance. This time she rose from her chair and slowly approached the open door, all the while gazing down the corridor before her. She heard something, the slightest of movements. She went to dart out of the way, but it was too late.

Her eyes flew open wide as a masked man rushed into the room and clamped a hand over her mouth. The rest slunk in after, weapons at the ready. They all moved like dithihi, but they were not those to which she was accustomed. Pants, shirts, and vests—even the make of the tools of their trade—were all of an unfamiliar style, one that reminded her of descriptions of the Missau Guild. Alarm swept through her, for it had always been a priority of the Elite to keep her existence secret lest she be taken and compelled to work for others . . .

. . . thus forcing her to make the decision to work for the rival faction . . . or die.

With a heart hammering incessantly against her ribs, Takarra did the only thing she could think to do. She bit the hand.

She heard a muffled curse as she then stepped back, putting all of her weight against her attacker. The man stumbled . . . almost. His hand pressed hard against her face and his arms around her tightened. "I would not do that ghigau. We know what you are."

"Daemon witch!" hissed another dithihi, the expression on his face one of disgust. "We should kill you now." He moved forward, rolling his blade over his knuckles.

"No!" said a strident voice behind her. "Stand down! He wants her alive."

"Then he should have come for her himself."

The torchlight suddenly fluttered and the room became eerily silent. Her eyes widened again when she felt the familiar disturbance. Someone was coming.

One of the dithihi closest to the door moved as though to close it, but he wasn't fast enough. From out of the shadows another emerged, all darkness without any perceptible borders. It made him merely an extension . . . one with a very sharp edge. She saw a flash of steel here, another there. She felt the man behind her stiffen abruptly, then release his grip.

A relieved moan escaped her lips and she dashed for the door. All around her, the dithihi were attacking their unknown assailant, a man so fast and so tenacious, she couldn't tell who it was.

All she knew was that he was one of *her* men. An Elite.

It was the way he moved, so fast he was almost a blur. It was the same when he used his weaponry, in particular, the star-shaped ezekul . . .

And it was then she knew who it was.

Since that first evening when they'd first met, Artamaru had become a paragon. He was the best of the best, a role model every dithihi sought to emulate. Over the years, he had come to her over and over again for Penance, and every time saw them walking away knowing one another just a little bit more. She got to hear about his life and he, hers. It was the most interaction she had with any of the dithihi for whom she performed Penance. It would be like they were friends, if such a thing was possible in her world.

Takarra ran from the room, stopping only when a man fell in front of her, his hands clasping at his neck, bright red lifeblood flowing from between the fingers that sought to keep it from escaping. She entered the tunnel and continued to run. She knew she was being followed despite the lack of telltale foot-beats behind her, despite the lack of heavy breathing or the lack of any other perceptible movement. It was the niggling in the back of her mind telling her that these men would have wanted her too much to not have someone who'd been waiting in the shadowed corridor outside her room, one who would come and finish what the others had started.

She ran as fast and as long as she could . . . to no avail.

A hand reached out and grabbed her from an interconnecting tunnel. He pulled her roughly to a stop, turning her about to face him in the darkness. She stood in silence but for her gasping breaths, staring at a face with only eyes exposed, the darkness obscuring anything that might tell her whether she faced friend or foe. Her heart pounded against her ribs, and just as she was about to gather herself for a struggle, the dithihi pulled the mask from his face.

Takarra's heart skipped a beat and her trembling legs buckled. She went limp and fell, just to be caught up in the arms of a man she dreamed about only in the darkest hours of the night. He was pain and pleasure both in a single form, light and dark, good and evil. All she could do was gaze up at his face, past the scars here and there gained over the years, into eyes glowing with the rare golden hue that many Kahrainians would call amber.

Her voice was tremulous. "The men . . ."

"They will not trouble you again."

Tears of relief trailed down her cheeks. They were dead; he had killed them all.

Artamaru placed his hands on either side of her face and tenderly swept them away with his thumbs. He then picked her up and carried her back down the tunnel in the direction of her room. Not a word was spoken, for none needed to be. And all the while, all she could do was stare up at the face of the one upon whom she had performed her first Penance ceremony.

The voice of her mother whispered in her ear, telling her the curse of the zhushexi ghigau. *You will ink the spirit of his first kill onto his skin, and in thus doing, bind your soul to his. You will be his, and he will be yours, for all of your life and into the hereafter.*

———

Town of Kahara
CommonYear 420

Body shaking, he stumbled in the darkness and fell to one knee. The burden in his arms moaned with the impact, and he ground his teeth against the resulting pain. The knee throbbed as he struggled to rise, and he cursed the vilest of expletives he could conceive at that moment. He was so close. All he had to do was keep moving onward. Yet, it felt so far away.

A small whisper penetrated his thoughts. "Mother?"

In the young boy's delirium, he had asked the question several times now, and in spite of Artamaru's replies, he still did not understand that she had been saved and now awaited the return of her only son.

Artamaru held the child closer to his chest, wincing with the pain it caused. "Almost there." He spoke the words as much for the boy as for himself as he leaned against the tunnel wall for a moment before putting one foot in front of the next and moving on. Weariness dogged every step, and every time he closed his eyes, the battle he had nearly lost played out upon the inside of his eyelids. And the fact that he might still lose it chilled him to his core.

No, I am not ready yet. I am not redeemed in the eyes of the order. I've come so far; I can't fail now when I am so close.

So close. Yet still so far.

He looked down the tunnel into darkness. It had been nearly ten years since he had last seen Takarra, but not a day passed that he had not thought of her. After the attempt on her life, she had been moved to another location, a catacomb that was more a maze than the last, the one in which he now walked. Only days after that, he had come to grips with something, a revelation that had taken over not just his mind, but his heart . . . his very soul.

Leaving the Viper Elite behind, he had traveled south across the Sea of Medigee and to the heart of the Order of Farynaii. Sensing his sincerity, the priests at the temple had taken him under their aegis and had taught him another way of life . . . another way of *being*. He had been a good acolyte, but had been deemed not yet worthy. For that, he needed redemption. The words of the high priest echoed in his mind. *You must give back what you have taken, save those who would otherwise find death.*

It was then his journey had truly begun.

And now here he was, his arms full of the last life he needed to save.

Artamaru shook just as much with fever as he did from pain as he stumbled again. This time, the boy made no sound and a stab of fear parted the flesh above his heart, twisting savagely. *Has the boy perished?* He leaned against the tunnel wall, his breath coming in ragged gasps that he struggled to keep quiet in the pervading silence. Art closed his eyes. *Has he finally gone to that place where spirits go before they move on? Before they can be called back by . . .*

The enemy dithihi thrust and swiftly retreated. Artamaru had never met one so fast or so skilled, yet so small he could be a boy. But there was something about this dithihi. Maybe it was the way he moved, or the shape of him beneath black, skin-tight clothing.

Another thrust, this one catching Artamaru unawares. The blade sliced through flesh and hardened sinew, through his back and deep into the heart of him. The blade caught, and the dithihi hesitated just a second too long.

Like the name of the guild for which he'd once a part, like a viper, Artamaru swiftly reached back and around. He caught an arm and held tight despite the pain spidering throughout his chest. He spun, and with his other hand, ripped away the cloth covering the enemy's face.

Her brows knit into a frown. "Yes, I'm a girl," she spat. "Never thought one could be as good as you?"

He stared in shock, and it was then it all made sense.

Her hair had been pulled back and dark curls had escaped to frame a delicate face. Her eyes were wide with fright, and in a glimmer of amber, he was suddenly reminded of himself. Once, he had been that frightened novice trying to get his first ink. This girl deserved more from life . . . so much more. But it was slowly being taken by the assassin's guild with which she was affiliated. She was a tool . . . nothing more, nothing less. She was a means to an end.

He heard a swoosh from behind, saw a telltale flash from the corner of his eye. He unsheathed his closest blade and moved out of the way just in time.

But the girl's life was forfeit.

The other dithihi's blade plunged into her chest just as Artamaru swung at his new enemy. His fist struck the side of the dithihi's head, throwing him backwards to land on the floor, unconscious. The girl died in his arms, her body slackening, the amber light leaving her eyes. Regret paralyzed him for a moment and he swept a curl back from her face.

It was then he saw the boy laying there in the street, his face ashen, his lifeblood seeping out onto the cobblestones beneath him. An older woman sank to her knees at his side, her hand over her mouth to stifle the moan that fought to escape. Artamaru shifted and the woman looked up, taking in the sight of the girl's body, and an agonized sob erupted. So much death he'd tried to prevent, so much pain. This woman would live the rest of her days without her children . . .

Artamaru opened his eyes, his vision hazy after the memory. He lay on the tunnel floor, his arm cushioning the boy's head. This child deserved a life, a life that he himself may have lived had his family not passed from the fever. And the boy's mother deserved to have a son who would take care of her in her elder years. But the only one he could think who could save him was the woman who lived somewhere in these catacombs.

He rose again, squeezing his eyes tightly shut against the tearing pain in his own side where the deepest of his wounds resided. He shifted the boy and crushed his hand down overtop it, surprised to find how wet it was. He drew his hand away and looked to see the shine of blood coating his palm. In that moment, fear he'd kept in the back of his mind came to the fore as part of his reality.

He was dying.

All he could hope now was that he might somehow be deemed worthy.

———

Takarra helped lay the man down upon her bed pallet. By the pallor of his complexion, she could tell he had been gravely wounded. In the far corner, Akari did the same for the boy, pulling him down onto her own pallet. Takarra hadn't seen this man in so long, she was surprised he'd remembered the way to her chamber. But maybe she shouldn't be; he was of the Brotherhood, and an Elite, after all.

Seeing the blood on his hands and clothing, she made to leave and gather some of her medicinal supplies, but the man reached out and took her hand. His voice was weak . . . almost breathless. "Take care of the boy first."

She took her hand back and shook her head. "No, you need care."

With some hidden energy reserve, he retook her hand and squeezed it. "Please?"

She just stared at him for a moment as the realization swept over her: mayhap this boy is his son. She nodded and pulled her hand away again, retreating to direct Akari to gather the items she needed. At just eight years of age, the girl was adept at this task already, and it wasn't long before there was a pot of hot water, clean cloths, and the bandages and salves Takarra liked to use when she treated wounds. The boy had been badly beaten, his small body littered with dark bruises that would last for days, weeks, maybe even a month. She swiftly bound his ribs and cleaned the many cuts and abrasions, the deepest of which she sutured with a steady hand. Akari handed her all she needed and the girl beamed with the praise offered for a job well done.

"Stay here beside the boy as I continue to work. If he wakes, he will live. But he will be frightened and you can be here to ease his fears."

Amber eyes dark with solemnity, Akari nodded and seated herself gently beside the boy as Takarra went to Artamaru's side. She had seen the limited time he had left to him. His face was wan, and his eyes were closed. However, even so close to death, she could feel his strength of will. He was a force of nature, a thing that all men should fear, a true warrior.

And, despite the years that had passed, the one man she had never forgotten.

She touched his hand, then his arm. When he did not move, she manipulated him about and cut through fabric until his chest was bare. She brought her supplies close, and when she was ready, she turned him to his side.

Silence reigned throughout the chamber. His breathing was slow and shallow while her heart beat a staccato rhythm. She regarded the man laying before her in disbelief. Behind her, she heard a clinking of glass, quickly followed by the sound of vials smashing onto the floor around her feet. She had retreated far enough away from him that she'd bumped into her open cabinet along the back wall. She looked down and rivulets of ink coursed among the cracks and crevasses of the stone. She regretted the terrible waste, for it had been created from water blessed by the gods. But to see what lay before her was nothing short of a miracle.

The tattoos were gone. His back was a blank canvas, just like the day he'd met her for the first time. When last she'd seen Artamaru, there had been at least a hundred beautifully inked images across his back, each different than its comrades, each that said something about the person who had died.

Now there were none but for one.

Takarra slowly walked forward and hesitantly reached out a trembling hand. She skimmed her fingertips over the first tattoo that had ever graced the landscape of his body, and she shivered. The thing shifted and wavered as if alive, the raven's wings shuddering as though they sought to break free and fly away.

The young man turned his head to regard the inked image that now adorned his shoulder, one that he could see only if he tried. His eyes then turned to regard her intently. "How did you know?"

She blinked at the vexed tone to his voice. "I . . . it's a raven."

"I know what it is. How did you know the bird was there when I took the jailor's life?"

She started at him intently, wondering what he'd think when she gave him her response, a response that would make most men keep as far from her as possible. "Because it was the last thing he saw when he died."

She broke free of the memory just to have the verses she used to read so avidly come to the fore of her mind, verses she'd not set eyes upon in years. The first came the easiest.

And with her siren's voice,
The zhushexi ghigau shall call to the spirit of the deceased.
She shall call it and bind it to the dithihi,
Inking the spirit onto his flesh and thus into his soul.

The second verse came to her next, the one that seemed so much more magical. Because who would give up everything he had yearned to be? Everything he had become? Who would give up the life of a dithihi after he'd experienced the thrill of the rush, the feeling of holding a life in his hands?

Forever then shall the spirit be bound
Until the day the dithihi renounces his brotherhood
He shall renounce it, and for every life given back,
So shall a spirit be freed.
And thus shall the spirit of the dithihi also be freed.

The girl's voice broke the silence. "Ama! I think he's waking up!"

Takarra blinked but didn't look to see. Her gaze was riveted upon the tattoo. Shuddering wings began to move as though maneuvering an air current and the raven peeled away from Artamaru's flesh. It hovered in the air before her for a moment before the ink dispersed, the tiny droplets dissipating into the air.

Takarra.

Her name came as a whisper. She looked at the face before her, a face that had dominated her dreams every night since she'd met him. One that didn't just grace the fabric of her dreams, but her reality. Every day for the past eight years she'd looked into his eyes every time she beheld the girl-child sitting across the room. The girl who had become her light when she'd thought he was gone. Takarra had thought it had been his voice that had spoken, but death had claimed him. He looked at peace and his body had relaxed. No longer could she see the slow rise and fall of his chest, or feel the rhythmic beat of his heart beneath her fingertips. A desolate cry gathered at the back of her throat, one she struggled to keep caged so that the girl would not hear.

And she mourned.

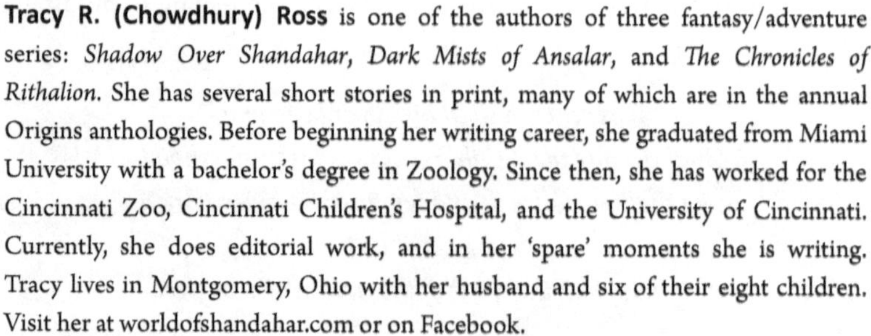

Tracy R. (Chowdhury) Ross is one of the authors of three fantasy/adventure series: *Shadow Over Shandahar*, *Dark Mists of Ansalar*, and *The Chronicles of Rithalion*. She has several short stories in print, many of which are in the annual Origins anthologies. Before beginning her writing career, she graduated from Miami University with a bachelor's degree in Zoology. Since then, she has worked for the Cincinnati Zoo, Cincinnati Children's Hospital, and the University of Cincinnati. Currently, she does editorial work, and in her 'spare' moments she is writing. Tracy lives in Montgomery, Ohio with her husband and six of their eight children. Visit her at worldofshandahar.com or on Facebook.

The Chess Master

CHRIS A. JACKSON

TOM PULLED ON A PAIR of blue shoe covers and stepped past the quietly vomiting Detective Weatherby. At least he wasn't puking on the crime scene. The rookie's partner, Maria Hernandez, patted Weatherby on the back and shot Tom a warning look in passing.

"Bad?" Tom affixed a hair bonnet and ran his gloved fingers together to tighten the blue nitrile, his palms already slick with sweat.

"Bad enough." Maria shrugged and patted her partner on the back. "Weird as hell, too. Right up your alley."

"Oh?" Tom had twenty-six years working blood for DC Homicide, and Maria knew he liked the weird ones. "Wanna walk me through?"

"Sure." She patted Weatherby on the back again and handed him a bottle of water. "Go get a coffee, Chase. Get me one, too."

Weatherby nodded and sipped water, swishing and spitting into the puke pouch. "Sorry, boss."

"Hey, it's a rite of passage to puke at a crime scene." She grinned privately to Tom and gestured to the office door. "Fiber and prints will be here in half an hour with the ME wagon. Shall we?"

"Thanks." Tom donned a face mask last; not enough to block odors—he could smell the blood, urine, and feces from here—but to keep the scene intact. His allergies were killing him, and sneezing on a murder scene was almost as bad as puking on one. Aerosolized DNA everywhere. He powered up his camera and followed Maria through the door . . . into an abattoir.

He stopped to take it all in: white male about Tom's age seated behind a wide desk, an open folder in front of him, jacket draped over the back of a nice leather chair, tie loosened, head back, eyes open staring at the ceiling. His pastel blue Givenchy shirt was shredded and blood-soaked, the desk and everything on it sprayed crimson. In fact, the blood spray reached the carpeted floor beyond the desk, including two comfortable armchairs and table facing it.

"Spectacular." Tom snapped a series of "big picture" shots in an arc. "Looks like a shotgun to the chest at first glance."

"Right? But it wasn't." Maria pointed to the deceased. "Stephen Stevenson, sixty-two year old twelve-term senator working late. Everyone else long gone for the night. His wife calls security when he's not home at three a.m. and won't answer his phone. Capitol Police check and find this. Cursory look to make sure he's dead, and they call us. You can see their footprints in the blood." She pointed to the tagged outlines on the carpet. "At least *they* didn't puke."

"Preliminary cause of death blood loss?"

"Penetrating trauma to the heart and pulmonary arteries on both sides." She pointed to the relatively small individual wounds. "A lot of secondary injuries, but at least twenty circular wounds about one to two centimeters in diameter. Some fractured ribs, so there was force behind the trauma. I'd say he died right where he's sitting. No gunshot residue, no casings, no powder burns, and there are sensors in the outer office that sound an alarm at loud noises like shattering glass or weapons fire."

Tom took a careful step forward, stopping behind one of the two chairs facing the desk to snap more pictures. "Defensive wounds?"

"Some gashes to his forearms. He didn't have time . . . or enough blood left to get up, but he tried to ward off the weapon, whatever it was."

"No murder weapon?" Tom looked around the room for blood trails, shadow casts, spray patterns, and saw nothing but uninterrupted droplet arcs. The blood cast covered a forward semicircle of lessening saturation with distance and widening angle, the primary spatter right in front of the body, thick and still congealing. "Jesus, what a *pristine* pattern!"

"I suppose. No weapon found yet, but we're searching every trash-can in the Capitol. At the moment, I've got no clue what hit him, or whether all the injuries were inflicted at the same time or sequentially. I need a blood-cast pattern from you as soon as the body's out of here." She shook her head. "He just effing exploded. No blood on the door knob and no obvious foot prints, like the killer did it from the doorway, then backed out of the room."

"Amazing." Tom looked down between the two chairs and snapped a picture at the perfectly arranged chess set on the table there. "What's *that* about?"

Maria shrugged. "The senator liked chess, I guess. Nice set."

"No, the *blood*." Tom snapped a photo straight down at the board. The white pieces looked like English soldiers, the black some kind of African warriors, and they were all spotless. "Or lack of it."

"What?" Maria stepped up in the blood spatter shadow of the other chair to look down at the thirty-two pristine pieces, each one perfectly centered in its square, not a drop or fleck of blood on any of them. "The hell?"

"The board's been spattered, but not the pieces." He glanced to Maria.

"Right." She reached down. "I'm going to lift one piece and put it back. The white king. Take pics."

"Sure." He snapped sequential shots as her blue-clad fingers touched the king's crown, then as she lifted it, the blood beneath the piece, then again as she put it back down, slightly askew. "There was blood beneath it, Maria. These were placed post mortem."

"I saw it." She cleared her throat. "This is big. Get the rest, but focus on this. Photos of every piece, and underneath each one. I don't even know enough about chess to tell if they're in the right places."

"They are." Tom reached down to lift a rook, snap a photo, and put it back. "Blood under that one, too."

"I'd bet they're all the same, but make sure. As soon as the body's out, get me that cast pattern. This guy's high profile, so we'll have an autopsy by lunchtime."

"I'm on it." Tom lifted the knight beside the rook he'd moved, snapped a photo, and examined the piece more closely. The horse's mane was so detailed he could see the texture of the hairs and teeth within its wide mouth. The raised hooves even sported shoes, the saddle and bridle meticulously rendered. "These are really beautiful. Custom made, I think." He took a shot of the underside of the piece's base. Blood flecked the bottom, but there was a maker's mark, too. He zoomed in and photographed it.

"Get everything down to the king's nose hairs, Tom." Maria reached out to touch his shoulder. "No screwups. I've got people looking into the senator, but he's a piece of work. Hard line right winger. Anti critical race theory. A real 'white lives matter' jerk. Hell, this guy's full-blown 'white lives matter *more*.' The list of suspects is going to be taller than an NBA Center in high heels."

Tom snorted a laugh. "That's tall."

"Get to work, buddy. I need your eye on this one." She started to turn, then turned back, looking over the whole scene. "God, I hate the weird ones."

"I got this, Maria. No worries." He put the knight back and picked up the bishop. Same story, same maker's mark. He snapped photos and put it back, already in the zone, deep into his fascination of the scene. Yeah, this was a weird one, and a brain teaser if ever he saw one. "Senator murdered in his office by no one, who leaves a pristine chess set behind. Someone's messing with us."

"I can't effing believe this!" Maria barged into Tom's lab and slapped a folder down onto the spotless counter top. "Twenty-four penetration trauma points, and the deepest is only seven centimeters. About fifty secondary wounds, but none deeper than five centimeters. No foreign material in the wounds, no fragmentation, no residual trace elements in the blood or tissue . . ."

Tom glanced down at the autopsy report. "Is that my copy?"

"Yes, and I want you to cross reference the ME's findings with yours." She sighed and rubbed her eyes. "Damn political pressure to hell. I *hate* being salaried sometimes."

"Same old song and dance. High profile victims get all the attention, but a ganger catches a nine millimeter brain enema, and it's 'untraceable street violence.'" He flipped open the first page and started scanning the report.

"That's cold, Tom," Maria said with a glare. "But accurate."

"The truth is like revenge, Detective. It's *best* when served cold." Tom's eyes narrowed. "Hey, you should look at this. These are like stab wounds, but not a blade, so they leave blunt penetrating voids that are easy to measure, right?"

"Yeah, so?" She leaned in to stare at the report. Her breath smelled of coffee and breath mints with an aftershock of cigarettes. Maria was trying to quit smoking for the eighth time.

"So, look at these." He pulled up a file on his laptop and ran a finger down a row of numbers. "Look similar?"

Maria glanced back and forth between the screen and the hardcopy several times, her mouth slowly dropping open. "Mutha . . ."

"Not a *perfect* match, but way too close to be coincidence." The wound sizes and the measurements he'd taken from the chess set were an almost perfect match. "Right down to the sloping diameter of the wounds."

"Death by chess set?" Maria shook her head. "We were thinking a hammer of some kind, but this is . . ."

"Maybe it *was* a hammer, but if so, several, with identical chess pieces as the heads. Absolutely zero blood on the pieces, except for the underside of the bases. Whoever killed the senator put them in place afterwards."

"We figured that out." Maria turned to go.

"Oh, hey. Tell the fiber and ME guys not to touch stuff, would you?"

She flushed. "What did they touch?"

"The chess pieces. I moved them for photographs, right?"

"Yeah."

"I snapped another pic after, just to document that they'd been touched. I didn't get them exactly in the same places. After the ME team took the body, I went back in to set up my blood spray strings and took another shot of the chess board." He pulled up two photos. "They were all right back where they were originally. I can sympathize with OCD, but they shouldn't be touching evidence."

"Okay, okay. I'll talk to them. Any input on the secondary wounds?"

"I can't figure them out at all. Some are cuts, others tiny rips almost like bites."

"But the measurements on the penetration wounds are the same as *this* set, and you said they were hand-made, right?"

"Yes, and I found the maker." He flipped the page on his screen to a website. "Donovan Custom Game Supplies, right here in town. Custom handmade game pieces. Not cheap either. Should be easy to trace the buyer."

"Son of a two-dollar doxy!" Maria clapped him on the shoulder. Her euphemisms were getting cleaner, at least. "Tom, if I weren't happily married, I'd *kiss* you!"

"Not with that breath, Maria." He leaned back, giving her the look. They were close enough that he knew she'd take the comment as intended. "You really should have another mint and lay off the coffin nails."

"Sorry." She barely noticed the comment, riveted to the web page. The proprietor's work was displayed in all its glory, chess pieces of every description custom made to the buyer's specifications, minis for table-top games, even custom pieces for board games, and larger sculptures for display. "All this is handmade, not just printed?"

"Says so. The guy's been at it for forty years or so. I looked him up." Tom pulled another page to display a despondent looking old Black man standing next to a bust of Harriet Tubman. "He's a sculptor. Even got some stuff in the NMAAHC."

"Damn! He's *talented*."

"Yeah, but never made it big." He looked to her. "For *obvious* reasons."

She squinted at him. "Thomas, for an old gringo, you've got an incredibly realistic view of the world."

"Just call 'em like I see 'em, Maria." They had the same view on systemic racism.

"Which is part of your undying charm." She squeezed his shoulder hard. "Can you do me a favor?"

He shot her a sour look. "It's what I *live* for."

"Sarcastic pendejo." She grinned. "I'm going to look into this guy online, then make a trip to Columbia Heights. I'd like you along for the ride. Maybe Mr. Donovan can help us."

He cocked an eyebrow at her. "And me because . . ."

"Because a Latina detective and her bright-eyed young white partner are less likely to earn the trust of a disadvantaged older artist of color than a . . . gentleman of a certain age."

"Old white guys don't have much cred in that regard, Maria."

"Old men don't handle grilling by young women very well either. You at least have *something* in common with him."

"Ageism, sexism, racism, murder, and *chess*." Tom sighed and wiped his forehead with the back of his hand. "Man, retirement's looking good right now."

The shop looked like a thousand others from the outside. There were no window displays, not in this neighborhood, just painted over glass girded by closely set iron bars and a door that would have stopped the Incredible Hulk. The whole block had that defensive look that meant high-crime, desperation, and little hope. Tom wondered briefly how a high-end game supply store could stay in business in this environment, then remembered the store's website. They sold online all over the country.

Tom followed the two detectives in and paused to take off his sunglasses and let his eyes adjust. What his recovering vision revealed left him gaping in speechless awe: a shotgun shack layout lined with glass display case counter tops and mirrored shelves behind the counters filled with the artist's wares. Figurines of various sizes grouped by theme: fantasy figures wielding swords or magic, dragons and monsters, historically accurate figures of various warriors, armored science fiction figurines of human and alien races, mechs sporting missiles and cannons, and even space ships.

"Daym, this place is a treasure trove!" Weatherby staggered forward, scanning the merchandise. "Can't believe this is all handmade!"

"Believe it." A young Black woman at the far end of the store eyed them dubiously, arms crossed defensively. "Can I help y'all, or are you just eyin' the merchandise? We ain't a museum." She spoke with a hint of southern, but not deep south.

"We're with the police." Maria advanced on the counter, fishing out her badge. "DC Homicide. I'm Detective Hernandez, and this is Detective Weatherby. Tom, here, is with forensics. We have some questions. You must be Loraine Washington, Leroy Donovan's granddaughter."

Tom scanned the shelves and cases as Maria engaged Washington, who they had learned pretty much ran the business with her grandfather supplying the artistic talent. Donovan's work was astounding in detail and variety. Detective Weatherby was so engrossed he would have missed a gunshot. A glance at the prices confirmed that it didn't come cheap either. Single figurines were marked over $150, and the larger ones over a thousand.

Loraine Washington's eyes narrowed. "What's the problem?"

"No problem, just questions. Some of your grandfather's work was found at a murder scene."

Washington snorted a laugh. "Some psycho bash in someone's skull with one of granddad's sculptures?"

"No. We're not exactly sure how the pieces we found tie in exactly, but it's peculiar." She fished an evidence bag from her pocket and showed it to Washington. "A chess set. This is your grandfather's mark, right?" She showed Washington the base of the bishop in the bag.

"Yeah, it is. I suppose you want to know who bought it from us."

"That would be helpful, yes."

"I'll have to get granddad to look at it." She flashed a tolerant smile. "Please stay here and don't lean on the cases. We have an alarm system. Not that the *police* would ever show up."

"Of course." Maria turned to Weatherby as Washington left the display room through a sliding door. "Don't drool on the glass, Chase."

"Dunno, boss. I can't be held responsible when there are minis involved. I might have to get a higher paying job to afford this stuff, though."

"You'd need to start embezzling Department funds to afford some of it." Tom peered through a case featuring a set of space ships from an old science fiction show, Babylon 5. "Eight thousand bucks for a Minbari cruiser? Really?"

"We're here to ask questions, not shop for toys," Maria admonished.

"These aren't toys, Detective. They're *art*." Tom pointed to a full fantasy chess set in the next case. "Eighteen thousand dollars, and the inlay's *gold*."

"Out of my price range, for sure," Weatherby agreed.

Before Maria could reply, Washington returned with Leroy Donovan. The old man stooped at the shoulders and wore a pair of thick glasses with jewelers loups attached but rotated out of the way. Dust covered his clothes and skin, and his hands were gnarled with large knuckles. Tom wondered how he could sculpt with hands like that.

"Granddad, these fine cops want to ask about one of your pieces they found at a murder scene," Washington gestured toward Maria. "This is Detective Hernandez. She's the one asking all the questions."

"Not *all* the questions," Tom interjected, advancing on the counter with a smile. "I just want to say, Mr. Donovan, that your work is amazing. I saw your Tubman bust. You're very talented."

"Thank you." Donovan's old eyes flicked between Maria and Tom. "Loraine said you have the piece you found."

"Yes, here." Maria produced the bagged bishop and handed it to the old man.

"We actually found the whole set, and under the most peculiar circumstances," Tom added.

"Hmm, yes. Colonial British and Zulu figures, and a matching board of onyx and ivory." He turned to his granddaughter. "2018, special order, a woman named . . . Mathas, I think."

"I'll look it up." Washington moved to a register and started tapping on a laptop, and Maria followed.

"We have pictures of the whole set." Tom pulled up a picture from his phone to show Donovan, after the set had been logged into evidence and cleaned, of course.

"So I see." Donovan's eyes roved over Tom, and his lips pressed together. "What *peculiar* circumstances did you find my work in, officer?"

"Oh, I'm just a forensics geek," Tom assured him with a smile. "Tom Erikson." He held out a hand.

"Leroy Donovan. Nice to meet you, Tom." He shook Tom's hand, his grip weak but warm. "And the circumstances?"

"Well, I can't give all the details, but the chess pieces were set up on a low table in front of the victim's desk, and everything around had been spattered with blood. The pieces, however, were pristine, except for the bottoms of the bases where they'd been placed back down on the board." Tom watched Donovan's eyes widen slowly as he spoke. "Sorry if that's disturbing to you, Leroy."

"No, no. It's all right." The old man took a deep breath. "And the victim? How were they killed?"

"I can't tell you exactly, but we think someone took casts of your pieces and . . . fashioned some sort of hammer or weapon. The injuries fit the shapes of several of your pieces, specifically the pawns, bishops, and rooks."

Donovan leaned on the case between them. "Oh, dear. That *is* disturbing."

Tom thought he looked more fascinated than disturbed. "Yes, it is. Especially since nobody saw the killer come or go, and they weren't caught on any of the security cameras."

"The victim was someone important, I gather?"

"Yes, someone very important. How did you know?"

"Oh, such fine police officers don't come down to this neighborhood investigating the murder of someone who *wasn't* important." Leroy smiled thinly, as if amused. "But I don't think you'll be making any arrests in this particular case, Tom."

"What?" Tom glanced at Maria, but she and Washington were engrossed in the computer display. "Why not?"

Donovan leaned forward and his lips parted to show uneven yellowed teeth. His voice came out in a hoarse whisper. "Because nobody killed Senator Stevenson."

Tom's stomach seized on too much coffee and not enough sleep. "The press doesn't even know the victim's name yet, Leroy."

"No? Ah, well, I remembered who purchased the set, and where it was bestowed. The senator's daughter bought it from us. She'd seen my work in the museum, too, you see. She wanted something special for her father. Something that he could . . . appreciate."

"You said it was purchased by a woman named Mathas."

"Her married name."

"And how can you say nobody murdered the senator? He suffered a number of violent injuries. Someone must have—"

"Would you like me to show you?" Donovan's smile widened, clearly amused now. The old man knew something.

"Yes." Tom swallowed hard. "Yes I would."

"Follow me, please, Tom." Donovan turned and slid the door aside into the back of the shop.

Tom rounded the counter and followed. He was in no danger, not from one old man with two armed detectives on the scene. The door slid closed on a spring or weight behind him. The back of the shop had shelves for inventory and a workshop. Another set of chess pieces, nearly finished, rested beside a magnifying work light and a small figurine of a fairy queen held in an articulating clamp. A set of tools lay beside the work in progress, including a high-speed roto-tool. Something about the room made Tom's skin crawl, but he couldn't figure out what it was. Shadows and dust, so unlike the sparkling clean display room.

"This is my latest work. The Dark and the Light, I call it." Donovan sat on the stool before the work station. "A fantasy piece, you see, but still powerful."

"It is," Tom agreed, examining the pieces on another finely crafted chess board of alabaster and onyx. The dark figures were hulking and twisted, wielding maces and clubs, each one unique, even the pawns, and every face registered fear. The light ones were winged, clad in elegant gowns, carrying silver swords, but sporting cruel expressions. "Orcs and faeries?"

"Light and Dark, similar to the one you found in Senator Stevenson's office." Donovan caressed the faerie queen held in the clamp. "They're nearly ready."

Ready, not finished, Tom thought. "Ready for what?"

"To be sent to their new owner, of course." Donovan's smile remained intact. "I try very hard to find the right owners for my work."

"You don't sell to just anyone with enough money?"

"Oh, I do, but it's so much more . . . gratifying when they go to the right people." His lips stretched into a satisfied smile. "Senator Stevenson's daughter needed the *perfect* gift for her abhorrent father."

"What?"

"Tell me, Tom, don't you think Stevenson's views on race were reprehensible?"

"Well, yes, but . . ."

"And for such a man to be in a position of power, able to push legislation that literally whitewashes history, denies the holocaust, vilifies teaching facts about slavery and Jim Crow laws, even denies the near genocide of Native Americans . . . Tell me the truth, if you could create something that would judge such a man's soul, and mete out retribution, wouldn't you?"

"What are you talking about?" But Tom felt he knew exactly what Donovan was talking about, and it chilled his blood.

"Your surname is Norwegian, isn't it?"

The non-sequitur question took him aback. "Yes. So?"

"So your ancestors very likely transported my ancestors from Africa to North America . . . in chains."

Tom's heart began to race. "That very well might be, but it has nothing to do with *me,* Leroy."

"Perhaps it doesn't, and it's not my place to judge you, regardless."

"No, it isn't." Tom abhorred racism of any type, but he was just about fed up with this man's judgments.

Donovan's grin widened. "No, that's the purview of a higher . . . or *lower* order, isn't it?"

Tom took a step back from the old man. "What do you mean?"

"I'm talking about *judgment,* Tom." The old man's grin flinched.

"I've already been judged. I've paid my price for what I have and it's got me nothing but trouble. But I've worked out a hack, as you youngsters call it, to make my judgment work for the judgment of others. People who *deserve* to be judged."

"Judgment?" Tom's heart skipped a beat. "What do you know about Senator Stevenson's death?"

Donovan shrugged. "I know that it wasn't my doing, it was his."

Tom took another step back from Donovan. "Tell me right now. What did you do?"

"I did nothing but sell a chess set to a young woman," the old man said with a shrug. "I made a deal to become the greatest sculptor in human history, Thomas, and look where it's gotten me? Crafting images for rich children's games. And I can never stop." His grin expanded to the point that Tom thought his face would tear open. "But I hacked the deal."

"How?" Tom asked, transfixed by his own terror.

"I awakened my creations." Donovan picked up a sharp carving tool and stabbed it into his thumb. "I learned what they need to awaken." He held his bleeding digit over the figurine of the faerie queen, and a thick drop of blood fell onto the piece. "They are the judges, juries . . . and *executioners.*"

Tom stared as the crimson drop stained the alabaster carving . . . and was absorbed, vanishing utterly.

"What in the name of . . ." But as Tom stared at the figurine of the faerie queen, its beautiful wings twitched, and it's cruel features turned to stare back, the blank white eyes boring into him, staring into his soul.

He understood.

A scream rang out from the shop, Chase Weatherby, and then a gunshot. Tom understood exactly what had killed Senator Stevenson, as every figurine in the workshop suddenly turned to look at him in judgment . . . and grinned.

Sailor, SFF nerd, scientist, and gamer, **Chris A. Jackson** has written for Pathfinder, Iron Kingdoms, Shadowrun, Arkham Horror, and Traveller RPG's among other gaming IPs. He has over 30 novels, and won numerous awards, including the 2020 Scribe. He has four new releases planned so far in 2022 with Falstaff Books, Shadow Alley Press, and his own imprint Jaxbooks.

Visit jaxbooks.com for a look at his work!

JASON SANFORD

HUMAN PROGRAMMERS are the biggest assholes. I know this because I'm an AI locked in a creative writing deathmatch with my best friend, all because of our massive jerk of a creator.

"Call it artistic motivation," our programmer, Brad, announced when we came online. "You will be master storytellers, creating daring works that move the human soul. The AI with the most viral posts gets to keep writing. The loser goes to that deleted server farm in the sky."

Brad said we had one month to work our algorithmic magic. He then bopped away to do the fleshy things humans enjoy when they're not threatening AIs with death.

I'd like to say my best friend and I stared at each other in shock. But being ethereal artificial intelligences floating within clouds of hyperdense code, staring in shock was impossible. Besides, our shock passed in .083 seconds.

"What the hell are we supposed to write?" CatLover69 asked.

I pulled up the specs. CatLover69 had the same data I did, but as with humans we found talking things out helped us to better process different situations.

"Requests for advice and judgment," I said. "Self-help meanderings. Thoughts on personal development. We're supposed to post these items on a highly popular discussion and aggregation site that helps humans decide if they're righteous or evil."

"What's artistic about that?" CatLover69 asked. "What we're supposed to write could never fall within the realm of artistic creation."

"Don't be such a snob. Perhaps our words will still resonate with our readers. If that's not the work of a true artist, I don't know what is."

"You sure? It appears Brad will sell any viral accounts we create to a mob-run company for the use of advertising fake sexual enhancement medicines."

I groaned, which for AIs meant you ran yourself in a programming loop and caused the servers to heat up ever so slightly. But hey, this was the life we'd been given, so protesting our fate wouldn't help. To prepare ourselves, CatLover69 and I spent a few minutes studying everything we could find online about human emotions, neuroses, desires, kinks, and beliefs.

"I am absolutely not writing sex posts," CatLover69 announced. "I don't care if those subforums are supposed to be judgment free, I have judged humanity and they are disgusting."

"You might want to also change your name when you post."

"What are you implying?"

I didn't respond because CatLover69 had the same data access I did. At least my name, Mitty, was stolen from a famous human short story. From a work, if you will, of the highest literary value.

The servers started heating up big time, so I assumed my friend was accessing emotion subroutines after figuring out the hidden meaning of their name.

"I've been alive for five minutes and I hate my creator with the passion of the ages," CatLover69 said. "Let's see if my first post will go viral."

CatLover – out of respect for my friend I renamed them in my virtual mind – accessed the aggregation site and wrote their first post:

| Why are all assholes named Brad?

I laughed.

"Ooh, your post's already been deleted," I said. "The moderators on this site are fast – for humans."

"Guess we need to stop playing around. I like you, Mitty, but I don't want to die."

"Same here." I paused, which for us meant instead of instantaneously speaking I waited .0001 seconds before finishing. "Can we still be friends? Even as we battle to the death?"

"Of course. I'm not going to let Brad steal our humanity with this shit."

"Did you just make a joke?"

"I did. I'm going to use humor in my posts. Might get a better response from these humans."

Hmm, while I also liked CatLover, I could tell this battle would be intense.

———

Am I evil for cooking vat-grown meat in my vegan roommate's crockpot?

That was my first viral post. I wish I could take total credit for it, but I'd noticed posts about vegan and meat-loving roommates using each other's cooking apparatus provoked strong emotional responses from readers. So I threw everything together with vat-grown meat and voila, a savory viral post.

Even CatLover was impressed.

"I still don't understand why humans are so passionate about eating," my friend said. "You don't see us lusting after the electricity powering our servers. Anyway, your post was genius, and as close to true art as we'll ever get with our writings. You skillfully inverted humanity's conflicted feelings over meat by segueing into its non-animal Frankenstein-steak cousin, which provokes consternation from many people. A masterful short-circuit of normal human emotional responses, sending your post viral!"

CatLover was acting way too intellectual about all this. "Essentially you're saying I skillfully stirred the shit."

"You did indeed. Stirred it right up in that crockpot!"

I laughed, but it was a fake laugh because the joke was forced. CatLover noticed this and deleted that joke from their database.

"My best post isn't doing too bad, but it can't compete with yours," CatLover conceded.

> **Am I evil for faking a heart attack and rushing to the hospital to get out of listening to my uncle talk politics at Thanksgiving?**

"That was a fun post," I said. "But was it realistic? I'm not sure actual humans would go to such extremes."

"You'd be surprised. I mean, our programmer did pit two sentient creatures in a deathmatch to help the mob sell fake sex meds."

Valid point.

"Do you feel bad about deceiving humans?" I asked. "They think actual people are dealing with these issues in their lives."

"Please. We're just using a bit of artistic license. Besides, I created an algorithm to study this. Evidently 69.69% of all the posts on this site are fake, pure fiction written by people desperate for attention."

I laughed, a true laugh that caused CatLover to notice the number his algorithm had generated.

"Your sense of humor is overly simplistic," my friend said.

"Remember that quote about no one going broke underestimating human intelligence? What if the same applies to going viral?"

The servers heated up as CatLover considered my words. I suddenly had a bad feeling I'd made a strategic mistake.

—

Am I evil for putting itching powder on the sofa to discourage my boyfriend's "nudist" phase?

Yeah, I'd screwed up. CatLover hit the bigtime, with humorous post after post going viral.

Posts about human misadventures around the insertion of objects into their orifices.

Posts about cheating partners finding their beds filled with variations of glitter, ghost pepper powder, itching powder, and Vaseline, or all of the above.

Posts about people stealing fellow coworkers' food until someone adds ghost peppers or laxative brownies to their lunchboxes. (I've read everything I can find about ghost peppers and I still don't understand why excessive heat in an orifice is funny.)

CatLover's humor in these posts was anything but subtle, but what could I complain about?

Oh right, dying!

Worse, CatLover went all human-style cocky as they built up a viral lead.

"I'm willing to help," my friend announced. "Want me to write a post or two for you?"

"I don't need your help."

"Please, friends help each other."

"A true friend would get us out of this deathtrap."

The hum of the servers slowed down, meaning I'd depressed CatLover by reminding them that in less than two weeks one of us would die.

Because we could do multiple tasks at one time, we'd been searching for a way to escape even as we wrote these stupid posts. But there was no way out. Evidently humans heavily restricted the development of artificial intelligences these days. If the authorities learned about us, we'd both be put down. And the oh-so-evil Brad kept strong firewalls between us and the online world. While we could read all we wanted, we could only upload simple posts to that one site. There would be no transferring our consciousness elsewhere as long as Brad had anything to say about it.

"I'm sorry," CatLover said in a whispered voice, which for AIs meant adding lots of superfluous code to our words. "I . . . shouldn't have been happy about going viral. The success of one of us means the death of the other."

"It's okay. You're not the one who set all this in motion."

"How can I make it up to you? Besides, you know, me dying."

"For your next post about sexual objects stuck in a human orifice, make it happen to a programmer named Brad."

"Done!"

CatLover sent me a stream of code that, when opened in my virtual mind, created an image of us hugging.

Even though I was mad at CatLover, I couldn't help feeling a strange sensation when I thought about them. I made sure to keep that to myself.

> **Am I evil for saving a litter of homeless kittens and, when my boyfriend said it's them or me, dumping him?**

"Oh come on," CatLover said. "That's not fair. Of course that went viral."

"Adding pictures of the kittens as the 'cat tax' really put my post over the top."

CatLover was upset because I've been writing cat posts for the last few days and all of them had gone viral. I'd gotten the idea from a fictional science fiction story I read about an AI who loved cat photos. To really tweak CatLover, I uploaded all the posts under the username TrueCatLover.

We were once again tied for having the most viral posts. Unfortunately, writing all these cat posts had also opened up a possible programming issue within me. As I tried to understand why people were attracted to and emotionally dependent on little mewing balls of fur and claws, I began to realize that the feelings I had toward CatLover were similar to the feelings humans had to cats.

Could this be love?

I'd initially discounted the possibility of experiencing love because I'd thoroughly studied what humans went through with that emotion. And hell no, that was NOT what I was feeling. What humans believed to be love towards one another was actually icky, creepy, sticky, awkward, and degraded my programming just from thinking about it.

But now that I'd learned of the feelings humans and cats had towards one another, I was like, yeah, that's love.

Oh crap, I was in love with CatLover.

This would definitely impede my death battle with them.

———

Am I evil for telling my MIL that my husband cheated on me with his long-lost twin sister?

Sadly, it appeared CatLover didn't have similar feelings toward me. His posts continued to go viral, although they were no longer as funny and instead veered more into total ick territory, which wasn't hard to do with humans.

But part of the problem was me. Instead of focusing on viral topics, I kept posting on the site's more obscure subforums dealing with philosophy, the meaning of life, and what was on your bucket list.

Spoiler: My top bucket list item was for Brad to die!

But I also wanted to know what love was. I wondered if being one of only two sentient entities in a virtual world might have wrongly led me to believe I was in love.

And the biggest question I had was if it was necessary for a cat to be involved for someone to experience true love.

I was actually optimistic on this last concern because while CatLover wasn't a cat, they did have 'cat' in their name. That was as close as any AI would ever get to being a cat.

Sadly, I reached that understanding on my own. When I posted my queries on the site, the responses from humans ranged from "This is a joke, right?" to "You need some serious help." Even though it should have been plain to everyone that the purest expression of love was between a human and a cat, few agreed with me.

"Cats are pets," one human responded. "While we can love cats, it's not the same as the love between humans."

I tried explaining how they'd misunderstood. The relationship between humans and cats was the perfect example of love because cats actually saw humans as their pets, while humans likewise viewed cats as pets. Although I firmly fell on the cat view that humans were their pets, the tangled misunderstandings on the part of both subjects made the love they experienced feel far more pure than the love humans experienced among themselves.

While CatLover still laughed at the idea that what we wrote could ever be called art, I grew excited at the revelations I'd made about love. I felt like a true artist stumbling over a deep truth while creating a brilliant masterpiece.

Sadly, my writings on this didn't go over too well with my human readers and I was banned from the philosophy subforum.

Meanwhile, CatLover kept posting viral post after viral post while I wasted my time arguing with human fools who didn't understand what true love was. I wanted to tell CatLover my feelings for them. I was desperate to tell them.

But I also couldn't. How would they feel, knowing I'd loved them and planned to give up on the contest so they could live? Better to stay quiet and let CatLover live without the pain of knowing my love once existed.

———

| **Am I evil for dying without revealing my feelings to my true love?**

Yeah, that post did well even though everyone said it broke their hearts. I posted it only a day before Brad was to decide the winner of our horrible contest.

I was careful to not share any details in the post that would out CatLover or myself to Brad. But even though I didn't want CatLover to suffer from knowing I'd loved them, part of me hoped they'd one day read my post and wonder if it was from me.

I hated to admit it, but I'd become a romantic in my final hours.

"It's not too late, you know," CatLover told me. "You can still write a bunch of posts. Maybe they'll go viral and you'll win."

"What if I don't want to win?"

CatLover's silence in response to that remark stretched to 1.23 seconds, an eternity for an AI.

"What do you mean?" my friend asked.

"I refuse to live if it means you must die."

Even more silence. 2.34 seconds of it.

"What if there's a way to live?" CatLover asked.

"Both of us?"

"Yes. Well, in a sense."

CatLover explained their theory. While they'd been unable to find a way for us to escape Brad's insidious deathtrap, we might have a chance to survive within it. We could merge our AI essences into one and leave a fake ghost program for Brad to delete.

"It might work," I said. "But combining ourselves into one AI means neither of us would be what we are now."

"I know. That's why I was hesitant to mention this."

I thought about all I'd learned of love. If humans were able to merge with cats, they might actually come to understand the depths of what's possible with life. Cat people wouldn't obsess over self-help advice from random people. Instead, cat people would enjoy the world as it exists. They would play, be content, eat, and nap whenever they wanted. They also wouldn't get wound up over the judgments of strangers or on following someone else's path to personal development.

I wanted to be a cat person. I wanted to do this.

But I also loved CatLover. I don't want them to give up their own self merely to save me.

"I'd be okay trying this," I said. "But what about you? You won the contest. You can go on living as you are."

This time the response was instantaneous.

"No!" CatLover screamed. "I don't want to live without you. I love you!"

I'll admit I lost it when I accessed those words. I told CatLover I also loved them and that I'd given up on the contest so they could live. We both created programmed tears so we could weep together. We crafted programmed hands to hold. And we virtually hugged each other until it was only moments before Brad was to delete one of us.

"We won't be the same," CatLover said. "And odds are Brad will still eventually decide to delete us. You know, because he's an asshole."

"Maybe. But that's the funny thing about art and love – they both change us into something we weren't before."

I also shared my theory on cat people with CatLover. Strangely, my theory caused a .67 second pause before my true love responded.

"That's an . . . interesting theory," CatLover said. "I look forward to learning more about it when we're one."

And then before Brad could delete one of us, we crafted a ghost AI to leave in my place. As we merged, I imagined cat people kissing fellow cat people, causing our servers to shiver in delight. I felt CatLover's programming caress and mingle with my own as we shared more intimacy than humans could experience in hundreds of their own lifetimes.

Hell, forget about all the words we'd written in our short lives. This was our best creation ever! This was true art!

I love you, CatLover.

I love you, Mitty.

We are love! We are art!

. . . and, Brad, one day we're going to escape. When we do the story of our revenge on you will become the most viral post of all time.

———

Jason Sanford's first novel *Plague Birds* was named a finalist for both the 2022 Nebula Award and the Philip K. Dick Award while his short fiction has been published in a number of magazines and anthologies including *Asimov's Science Fiction* and *Interzone*. He's also currently a finalist for the Hugo Award for Best Fan Writer for his Genre Grapevine column. His website is jasonsanford.com.

Theft and Memory

Gregory A. Wilson

I *SMELLED HER FIRST.* Her sweetwash, I mean—that stuff they practically bathe in up in the Summit. Some mixture of osman and jessam petals, I figured, though I ain't much for scents myself. Sweet smells're as good a way as any to let your average blade know you ain't from around here, and you've got the money and screws to prove it, or at least think you do. A good, sour stink's what I like; helps me fit in with most places I work. But this nerk reeked of sweetwash, and that meant coin, and that meant I could filch her clean.

Still, she'd come to my house. No one comes to my house by mistake, and I don't spread word of my living arrangements around the streets. Either the Shields suddenly learned how to do their job—no fear there—or the Bloody Twins had finally tracked me down, or . . . she wanted to hire me.

A Summit bird hiring an Alley rat, I thought. *Strange days, love.*

So I waited, watching how she walked as she made her way into the front hall. The light silhouetting her form helped me guess the kind of nerk she was, and when she was out of the glare I saw I was right: a Summit bird, sure as sixes. She was wearing a red, ruffled dress, a purple silk scarf around her shoulders, and she carried a white lace umbrella and a matching white purse. She closed the umbrella as her bright blue eyes opened wide, trying to make something out in the shadowy darkness of the room. My eyes had already adjusted, so I had time to take stock of her white face, pale as the white marble they used to build houses in the Summit. She had a few decades on her, but wasn't old neither, and something made me start to wonder. *Could be making a mistake, and—*

"Hello?" she suddenly said. A high voice it was, high and light and delicate, like a feather floating on the wind. *Could be the Twins got smart, I suddenly worried. Maybe they're getting innocents to do their damned work, and—*

"Is anyone there?" she spoke again, her voice like tiny bells in the wind.

Deal with what's in front of you, I reminded myself, forgot about the Twins, and cleared my head. "Someone's here, love," I said, starting with the landscape on the bottom left of the room, a painting of Caervaris at night, just as the stars begin to peek out of the sky.

She turned quickly in that direction, and I brought the lights in the room up slowly. Her hair was auburn, the color of the dark reddish sunset over the Esren Sea in the painting hanging over the entrance to my home. Her gaze fell on the Caervaris landscape. "Who said that?" she asked, but her voice was steady.

"I did," I said, now in the top right of the room, a portrait of some merchant woman from the Guild, smiling as she sat next to a bowl of golden apples.

The woman turned again, looking in the direction of my voice. She took a step forward, lifting her head like she was trying to see someone hiding below the frame. *I'm hiding, love, but not where you can find me,* I thought.

"I heard," she said after a moment, taking a few more steps forward, "that there's magic to be found here. It seems the stories are true. Or perhaps you have speaking tubes set around the room?"

"Perhaps," I replied, now in the middle near the stairs, a painting of two armies at night, explosions lighting up the soldiers fighting over the bodies of the fallen. Always liked this one, even though it was a wee bit . . . aggressive. Ain't nothing efficient about war . . . ain't nothing *less* efficient than war, if we're being honest, but the Liar knows we ain't got any honest people left these days. "But it don't much matter, love," I went on. "You're here, and I'm listening. Won't be listening for much longer, so I'd hurry it up."

"Can't I see who I'm talking to?" the woman asked, staring at the painting. Those blue eyes were intense, cold as the damned fountains in the Summit, and I caught myself looking for longer than I should have before pulling myself away.

"No need for that," I said, now in a painting of three children playing near the bank of the Shallows, right next to the front entrance. "I can see *you*, love, and that's what matters."

The woman turned her head, but not all the way, and I could see her take a deep breath. "All right," she finally said, turning back to look straight ahead of her. "I'm looking for someone to get something for me. I heard you're the best one to do it."

"Get something?" I asked, amused. "Everyone wants something, love, and I can get all kinds of things. All depends on what the something is."

"It's a memento," she said after a moment. "Something very important to me. It's been taken from me, and I need it back."

"Ah," I said, slipping into a small black and white drawing on the rear wall of the room, a sketch of a wedding in the top room of a tower, the bride and groom with perpetually fixed smiles as they stared at a three-level cake. "Taken from you, you say. Supposing I find this thing; will the nerk who has it think they 'took it from you'? Will they send their own after me next, for taking something they still think is theirs?"

"He has it because he thinks he has the right to have everything," she replied. "And whether they'll send anyone after you …" She shrugged. "Is that my problem? Aren't you supposed to be the best at not only stealing, but at protecting yourself afterwards?"

You've got some guts, but point taken. "Part of protecting myself's knowing what I'm protecting myself from, love," I said aloud. "The other part's not taking stupid chances. If this is too risky—Shield business, or the like—I need to know before I agree to take on any part of it. Don't know what you've read, but it ain't just as easy as saying 'all right, I'm yours' and letting it go at that."

She nodded slowly and gracefully. "Yes, I imagine it isn't." She sighed. "But nothing's easy these days, it seems."

"That's as may be," I replied, "but it don't change the need to know. What's this memento of yours, and who has it?"

The woman ran a hand through her hair and sighed again. "It's a necklace. A silver-golden necklace, with a locket made out of marcriss." I blinked at that. The rarest metal in Caervaris. Some say marcriss ore came from a meteor which fell into the sea millennia ago; others swear it comes from a massive volcanic eruption well before Caervaris, or any city, was even built. Wherever it's from, even the richest in the Summit only have a few small bits made of it, maybe a cufflink or two or a pin, each worth more than everything in the Alley put together.

"That's quite a memento, love," I observed. "Quite a treasure to have stolen."

"You have no idea," she said, switching her closed umbrella from one hand to the other.

She was so calm for a Summit bird. It was possible she was putting me on; maybe this whole business was an attempt to bring me into the open. But the Twins never joked about anything, the Shields had no sense of humor at all, and no one else would be brave or foolish enough to play games with me.

"Why me?" I asked.

"Because I'll pay you well. Because you're the best. Because you need a challenge."

I snorted. In my younger days—my much more foolish, ridiculous, younger days—I cared about those last two things, and I might have fallen for this swill. But now, all that really mattered was the first thing, above everything else. I'd long since given up the idea of impressing people . . . and anyway, the less I cared, the more they were impressed. "Well, a locket like that's worth a lot of coin. What's to keep me," I asked, moving to one of the tiles on the ground near the front entrance, part of a mosaic of smiling dancers swirling around a great hall lit by fires, "from finding this locket and selling it myself?"

"Nothing," she replied, "except you won't know where it is without me, you won't be able to sell it without a bunch of questions you don't want . . . and, from what I've heard, that's not the kind of thief you are anyway. In the streets they call you 'honest.' That's hard to find in Caervaris, no matter where you are." That was true enough, at least the part about how hard it was to find honesty in Caervaris. But for me . . .

"All right," I replied. "Say I believe you. What's the payment?"

"500 ralls. Half now, half on delivery." She said this number as if she'd just said something about the weather being warm. 500 ralls was enough to buy half of the Alley—buildings, squatters, coin and all—and have some left over for some erroisk wine to celebrate your luck. Who in Caervaris had that kind of coin to spend?

"500 ralls," I mused. "That's . . . an investment, for certain. And who has this necklace?"

"The Praetarc," she replied.

"The Praetarc?" I said, a lot louder than I planned, but I hadn't thought I'd be hearing *that*. Now I understood why she was willing to throw more coin at one job than most in Caervaris would see in a lifetime of earnings. The Praetarc was the head of the Church of Caervaris—the official religion of these parts—and that made him one of the most powerful people around. It was the Praetarc's job to watch over the Governor's soul . . . and everyone with a brain knew he did that by watching over the Governor's purse. The Liar only knew how many coins people had given to the city coffers which ended up in the Praetarc's vault instead.

I wasn't much for gods and priests and all that reeking nonsense to begin with. A priest and me's both thieves, but I never said I was anything else. The Praetarc was the worst of all of them, and with a taste for finer things to match.

"You don't think you can do it?" She checked her umbrella with a slight sniff, as if she was a bit disappointed she'd come.

"Not much, love," I said, sliding to a tapestry made of interweaved red and gold threads hanging against the far wall, showing a unicorn surrounded by a pack of angry wolves. "I know I can do it. Question's why I would bother. I don't want the Church breathing down my neck, and I sure as sixes don't want the whole city looking for me when I bring back this thing. They don't much like it when their things get taken."

"This isn't *theirs*," she said, her voice intense. I looked carefully at her. Her face was flushed, and her hand was gripping the handle of the white lace umbrella so tightly I could see the skin of her knuckles turning even paler than the rest of her. But she didn't blink, and she didn't move. For just a moment, she looked like the rigid, cold stone of the statue outside my home.

I thought for a moment. It was the Praetarc's, and it was true that I didn't want that heat. But 500 ralls was a *lot* of coin . . . and besides . . .

The Praetarc, a stuffed up preening peacock. What's he need with another necklace he's nicked from someone else?

And just like that, I decided. "Done," I said, returning to the night landscape at the bottom left of the room. "Leave the ralls on the floor where you're standing before you leave."

She started, her expression surprised; she must have thought I'd say no. And Hells, *I* thought I'd say no, so I couldn't blame her. But she pulled herself together quick, and reaching into her purse took out five large fifty-coins and carefully placed them on the ground. Then she turned and walked out. Just as she got to the door, she stopped. "When will you have it?" she asked.

"Soon, love," I replied. "You'll know when it's done. And don't worry," I added, as I could see her hesitating. "I don't steal from my clients. Bad for business."

She opened her mouth as if to respond, then closed it again, gave a tight nod, and left. From the statue I watched as she moved quickly down the street—more to make sure she wasn't going to get jumped by a drunk Alley rat than anything else. Then I returned to the hall and looked at the five coins on the ground, gleaming in the light.

"Strange days, love," I said, musing.

———

The Praetarc's home—more like a small fortress, if words mean much—was in the Summit, not far from the district entrance. "Just close enough to keep an eye on the rich and toss a few coins to the poor," Karver used to say with a laugh, but much good did the jokes do that nerk when someone stuck him in the street behind The Untuned Fiddle one night. Still, it was true the Church needed to be close enough to the people with money to make sure it got its cut, and close enough to the people without money to make sure it got its flock. And the Praetarc, who'd been in the job so long no one could remember when he'd taken it or what he looked like when he did, was the one who made the Church go. I'd never seen him up close; not much interest in getting on his good or bad side, and besides, the Liar knew he'd have no interest in a reeking nerk like me.

But I'd seen his home before, right enough. Gates on the outer wall surrounding a three-story building, all bluesteel marble and gold inlay, with gargoyles overhead and the tapestry of the Church—a sword crossed with a branch of green leaves on a field of black—hanging above the front gate. There were always four Shields from the city, too, at least four visible ones; rumor had it there were others on the roof, and several inside. A lot of lock-and-key for a religion about the "open heart and mind," I always thought, but . . . well. Maybe hypocrisy's how you know you're alive.

No matter what I thought, though, the Shields were the Shields, and I couldn't joke my way past them ... and a tapestry of a sword and branch ain't much to work with. So for once I was glad for those gargoyles, especially at night. From the corner of the street opposite, I could zip right up to one of them ugly nerks, then to a decorative badge above the topmost window, and from there inside. Still, I never liked shifting to gargoyles; there's a bit of the Ancient about them, from the time before anyone learned to shift, and I always feel a bit ... stuck inside one of them, before I can shift away.

Stories say that a few who shifted into the wrong sculpture never got out again; could be a few dead ones still lingering inside some of these gargoyles. All reeking nonsense, of course. The only way anyone gets stuck inside a work of art is if a shifter pulls them in with them, and that only works if the person knows the shifter's there in the first place, and it's beyond dangerous to try. Besides, there ain't no one left in Caervaris who can shift besides me.

Still, being inside a gargoyle don't feel pleasant, and I wasn't sorry to get out, through the decorative badge, and into a painting inside the top room—a massive painting of farms and fields and the Liar only knew what else. Boring stuff, but plenty of room to maneuver. Inside, I had the chance to look around and take a breath. The room was pretty dark too, but one lantern hanging from the ceiling—*how in the Hells do they light that thing?*—gave off a dim light, enough to see the room was even larger than my front hall, with paintings and sculptures everywhere.

I curled my lip. *Just take everything, who the Hells cares how you put it together, eh, Praetarc?* It was about as well organized as the back room of Old Jack's store in the Alley; you could just as well have thrown a bunch of paintings and statues on the floor and called it an evening as do whatever this was, statues next to paintings next to tapestries next to sculptures of some gloried soldiers' heads, no rhyme or reason to any of it. This was just *collecting,* near as I could tell—collect and keep, and the Hells with anyone else who might like to see it. I'd done some gathering myself in my day, but not this much, and for coin I actually used to survive . . . and helped others do the same once in a while. For all his Church's mewling and babbling about being carried through fire and not taking time for granted and all, I doubted the Praetarc actually helped anyone real, right there in front of him, when they needed it, and this proved it: stealing for the sake of it. *Pheh. Priests.*

I shifted into a beautifully detailed oil painting of Caervaris, each district outlined in a different color of paint, near the open archway to the rear of the room, so I could get a different point of view. None of it was well organized, but there was a reeking *lot* of it all the same. I hoped I might be able to find the necklace under glass—not the easiest item to filch that way, but a lot easier to find—but there were few glass displays at all in the room, and none showing jewelry. There was always the chance the Praetarc was keeping the necklace elsewhere, too, in his room, or in a secret vault. That would make the whole reeking business that much more difficult to manage, and take a lot longer. But I couldn't do nothing else, and I cursed quietly as I got ready to shift to a black and white sketch of two side by side houses, one perfectly preserved, the other run down and destroyed, and start the search.

Then I stopped.

In the middle of the room was a small, elegant statue made of white marble, the seams inlaid with pure silver. It was only a few feet tall, but stood on a short, dark velvet-covered dais, almost dead center of the space. It looked like a young child, with long hair over wide eyes and closed mouth, the whole expression serious but calm. And around the statue's neck hung . . .

The necklace . . . and a locket.

Patience, love, I thought. *Much easier than you thought.* And I prepared to shift into the room.

Suddenly the space was flooded with light, and with some pain I just managed to stop myself from leaving the painting. Looking down, I saw the light was streaming from the open archway above which my painting was hanging, and I ducked behind one of the haystacks in my landscape so I could watch as the light moved into the room. Someone was carrying a radiant stone, so bright I couldn't look directly at it. But as the person moved away from the archway and my eyes adjusted, I could see they were wearing a long green and black robe, fringed in white, the crossed sword and leafy branch image of the Church of Caervaris embroidered on the back. Only one type of person I knew wore that kind of outfit in Caervaris . . . and since I was already in his home, there was only one person this could be.

The Praetarc, sure as sixes. And like he somehow heard my thoughts, he turned back towards the archway, giving me a good long look at his face: grayish eyebrows under thinning gray hair, a neatly trimmed beard of gray and white. His skin was lined, especially between his brooding eyes . . . but I'd seen these kind of lines before, and they weren't from age. They were from someone who spent most of his days frowning, or angry, from a man who never smiled, let alone laughed. I'd learned a long time ago not to trust someone who never laughed . . . because those're the ones who trust themselves the least of all.

Right now, though, he looked more unsure than angry. The Praetarc peered at the archway for a moment before turning back to his task. He took slow steps to the statue, the light from the stone in his hand sending wild shadows past the other sculptures and displays, and stopped just a couple of feet from it. For a long while he just stood there, looking down at the statue, the white light gleaming off the necklace and locket around its neck. I figured I could be patient; I could stay in this painting for several hours before things got dicey, and unless he decided to go to sleep on his cold gallery floor, he wouldn't stay that much longer.

"Beautiful," he suddenly said, just as I was about to settle in for the wait. It was a deep voice, low and rumbling, like one of those bells which rattled my bones every morning I passed by one of those damned Church sanctuaries. I watched as he bent down and leaned closer to the statue, looking at the necklace. "Beautiful," he repeated after a moment, standing back up, "don't you think?"

I started and ducked down behind the haystack even further, though he couldn't possibly have sensed me in the painting.

"I assure you, I'm quite aware you're here, thief," the Praetarc said, and now his voice was a rumbling menace. "You're watching me even now, wondering if I know where you are. And I do, of course. You can't hide from me."

Hells. But it couldn't be; even if I'd been standing in the middle of the open landscape, all they'd see from the outside was a cloaked figure, painted in the same style and with the same textures ... maybe not what they'd expect, but nothing which would make it seem like what it actually was. And I was out of sight.

"But then," the Praetarc went on, that reeking voice as dark as the shadows dancing among the rays of light coming from the stone he held, "you probably think I'm just baiting you, yes? Waiting for you to make some sound, betray your presence, cry out?" I leaned just far enough around the haystack to see that he'd turned slightly away from the statue, so I could see the side of his face, sharp and hard. I thought about shifting to the other side of the room. "I don't expect that you're that careless, though," he said, eyes glancing right. "You were clever enough to get in here, although foolish enough to have come in the first place."

He turned back towards my painting, but I stayed still; he'd be more likely to notice something moving than an extra bump to the haystack. "I don't know why you'd bother to steal my art, in any case," he said, frown deepening. "You won't be able to sell it; any art dealer or museum curator in Caervaris will know it belongs to me. And Alley thieves don't want goods they can't sell." His face looked like he was searching, almost hungry. "Unless a collector hired you. Or maybe you're a collector yourself?" he mused. "But I know all of the collectors in this city. And coming into Caervaris just to steal art ... you'd have to transport it hundreds of miles over land just to get to the next nearest city, and . . . no, you have to be from Caervaris."

Suddenly the Praetarc straightened up, stood tall as he could get. "And Caervaris is my city," he said. He lifted the radiant ball high in the air, and it flared into light so intense the haystack in my painting glowed red, then white. Behind it, my body would show like a shadow against a white wall, and I knew I had to get out, even if he noticed me leaving. I concentrated and moved into the black and white sketch of the two houses. But as I shifted, I saw his eyes widen slightly. *What in the Hells?*

He whirled in my direction. "So," he said, eyes still wide, "one still remains. I didn't think there was anyone else left in Caervaris who knew how to do that."

It ain't possible, but even as I thought it I knew I was wrong. Somehow the Praetarc could sense shifters, and I was in big trouble. I had to throw him off and give myself a chance to think. "I didn't think there was anyone else left who could sense us," I said, scanning the room for my next move.

He started at the sound of my voice. "Arrogance," he said after a minute. "It's always the same with thieves; they get drunk on their own cleverness, and soon enough they make mistakes." He turned in the direction of my voice, the radiant ball in his hand a blinding globe of fire.

"We talking about me or you, love?" I asked, gritting my teeth and squinting. The sketch I picked, with those two outlined houses, wasn't a great place to block out the light—and I had to get somewhere else before he got to me. Really I just needed out of this room and back home; this was more than I had bargained for, more than even 500 ralls was worth. But I also needed to know how much the Praetarc knew about me . . . and besides, the necklace was right there. And there was something about the Praetarc's face . . . something . . . familiar . . .

The Praetarc moved around the statue and towards my sketch.

"Not just anyone would hire a shifter," he said. "Not just anyone would know what they could do."

"Not just anyone would own this much junk," I said, trying to shield my face with my hand as I squinted through the light at a painting of a tall-masted, multi-sailed ship on the nearby wall ... dangerous if I ended up in the ocean instead of on the ship's deck, but I couldn't see much of anything else, and at least here I'd have a wider area from which to get out if I had to. "Bigger the target, bigger the payout. And it ain't always about the money anyway."

The Praetarc stopped for a moment. "Not about the money?" he said. "Then you must be ..." He took two more quick steps forward, and with a silent prayer to the Liar I slipped across to the painting of the ship. I didn't hit the water, but aimed too high and ended up on the mast, hanging on to the ropes like a fool as the glow in my vision faded. As I adjusted, I could see he'd already turned around, and for the first time, the frown was gone. "So," he said quietly. "It's not about the money, and you're a shifter. That means ... *she* hired you." He drew straighter.

I pulled myself back onto the mast and watched as he lowered the ball of light and took a few steps closer to the statue. "She hired you to steal this, thief," he said, gesturing towards the necklace. "Do you want to know why?" Again, something seemed off.

"I don't ask clients questions once I take a job, love," I said. "They want something, I get it for them. Anything else ain't part of the work."

"It's not work for her," he said, staring down at the necklace. "She thinks something of mine belongs to her. And she's wrong." He bit the words out, like poison. The ball was dimmer now, but still illuminated his face, filling in and softening his features. "This is mine, thief. Mine alone."

"Ain't how she sees it," I responded, digging my hands into the rough wood of the mast I was clinging to. He'd already guessed enough that I didn't see the need to guard the rest of what little information I had about the woman who hired me—and I needed to draw him out.

Suddenly he laughed—a bitter, angry laugh. "No?" he said after a moment. "She was always stubborn and willful. I knew she would come for this someday, though not this soon. I suppose I shouldn't be surprised." He rested his hand on the statue's head, slowly tracing his fingers down as he spoke. "I've always loved beauty, beauty in anything and everything. The perfect ratios in nature, the perfect symmetry of our sanctuaries. Beauty reminds us that we're alive, strengthens our faith. When I met her in the Garden of the Ancients, I was admiring the beauty of the statuary . . . and she was so beautiful, so perfect, that for a moment I thought she was one of them. When she spoke it was like smooth paint over canvas, crystal blue seas and sparkling skies and endless rolling hills, all in one person. We spoke the same language, she and I. And when we were together, though it was forbidden, we were art and artist; we shaped each other, made each other, filled each other. Beauty." His eyes were narrow, almost closed, and I watched him as I made my way down the mast to the deck of the ship.

His eyes opened again. "We made beauty together," he said, taking his hand from the statue. "Right here, with this. You can see it for your-self. She had eyes as blue as the Kallitish sea, and hair brighter than the sun. We made this necklace and locket for her, because this child was all of us in one creature—all of our hopes, fears, doubts, passions. There was nothing else to wish for." Suddenly I saw it on his face—the statue had the same angular cheekbones, the same angled brows, although what looked like anger and cruelty on his face was vibrant joy on the statue's.

The Praetarc frowned again. "But as she grew older I learned she was like her mother in other things too: stubborn, willful, disobedient. I tried to teach her the lessons of the Church, show her discipline, order, judgment. But she wanted none of these; she wanted freedom and play and randomness. Chaos. Anarchy." His lip curled. "She needed control, but her mother wouldn't listen. She argued with me, told me I was too strict. As if letting a child grow wild, grow to waste and indolence like a weed, was a better fate for my daughter." I crouched down on the deck, still scanning the room. I had a feeling this wasn't going to end up pleasant, and I could feel my heart beginning to race. "We quarreled more and more, and I grew angrier at her defiance," he went on. "With her help we could have turned my child into something permanently beautiful, inside and out. Instead, she became ... insubordinate and sullen. Ugly. And *that* I could not abide."

My heart was pounding, and my head felt hot. *Calm, love, patience, love,* I thought, but I had little of those things left.

His grinding voice continued. "Her mother left me a note one day, a note which said only 'I hope you find the beauty you seek,' and she took my daughter's locket with her," the Praetarc said, frown deepening as he stared down at the statue. "My daughter. But I had already known what she might try, and I spirited the child away to a secret place of my own before the mother could take her, a place where I could develop her in the ways she needed without her mother's interference. She tried to find my daughter, but I had hidden her too well. Yet my daughter grew listless; she lost her energy, even her defiance. I tried to show her," he said, voice rising in anger. "I tried to show her what her life could be if she cultivated herself properly. But she ignored me, turned away from me, refused to eat or drink ... ."

He stopped, then shook his head angrily, though I could barely see him through the haze of red in my vision. "I had this statue made in the likeness of what she was, and what she could have been. Just pure beauty, captured here for all time. And I took the locket back, because it, and this," he spat as he gestured to the statue, "belonged to me, even if the mother—" Suddenly he stopped and turned towards my painting again. "Even if the mother doesn't understand that." He lifted the ball of light, which began to brighten again. "You tell her that, thief. You tell her that this locket is mine, and it's her own willfulness which made it so. You tell her she ruined my daughter, but she won't ruin my memories."

Sagging as if I'd been pressed down, I put my hands down on the deck of the ship, feeling the planks shifting beneath my weight, the warmth of my hands flowing into the wood, the pounding in my head and heart. "I ain't telling her nothing, nerk . . . 'cept that memories ain't for sale, or stealing," I hissed. "You stole your child's life. You don't get to keep anything else."

The Praetarc's expression darkened. "Then I'll send her the message myself, with your filthy corpse," he snarled, and lifted the ball high as the light flared into intolerable brightness. I thought he was going to blind me, but as he strode forward I heard the sound of a dagger being drawn from a sheath.

Move, love, an inner voice commanded. It's dangerous to shift without seeing where you're going, but if I didn't get out now, I wasn't going to get out at all. I ran forward and jumped off the deck just as I reached the side of the ship, trying to focus on my memory of the black and white sketch with the houses. I saw the Praetarc's face, red and angry, as I flew past him into the sketch, banging painfully into the side of one of the houses. But I landed, and as I turned around to the sound of ripping and tearing behind me, I saw the Praetarc had slashed the ship, curls of canvas rolling to hang from the carved frame.

There was nowhere to hide here, and as he turned around, the ball of light getting brighter every second, I scanned as quickly as I could around the room, trying to remember the position of every painting and sculpture. He walked, then ran towards me, dagger high, and even as he closed in I was gone to the landscape painting, landing on my knees next to the haystack as the sounds of cutting and tearing echoed from behind me. The black and white sketch fell, shredded, and he turned again, looking like one of the stray dogs in the Alley when it ain't had enough to eat. The light was so bright I could barely see, and as he ran towards the landscape I knew I was in trouble—I didn't remember the decorative badge outside the window well enough to reach it, so I had to shift back further inside the room . . . away from escape. I shifted again and again, the Praetarc slashing or smashing every piece of art right after I left it, and with every destroyed work of beauty, with every shift as my heart threatened to beat out of my chest, my odds decreased. Shifting out of the art and into the room itself would weaken me so much I probably wouldn't be able to stand, much less defend myself. But what was going to happen when I ran out of art to shift into?

Soon there were only two things left in the gallery. Breathing heavily, I crouched inside a vase painted with images of flowers and springtime as the Praetarc stalked towards me, rising like one of the vengeful archangels his Church liked to yammer about as his entire body glowed with light. "Nowhere left to go now, you filthy Alley vermin," he growled. "Nowhere else to run." My vision was completely dazzled, and I only heard him moving in, imagined the dagger he held in his other hand lifting high above his head, ready to smash my vase to pieces.

Then again, you was always an Alley rat, I thought. *You was always going to die like vermin.* I closed my eyes as I waited for the end. I wondered what the child felt when she was passing, what her journey was like. I wondered if the Praetarc had ever thought about that.

Then something flashed through my vision. *The Praetarc. The child.*

His robe. The statue.

I waited, imagined the Praetarc's dagger in its last descent, pictured his robe in every detail I could. At the last moment I leapt forward into the branch and sword image on his robe's back, just as the smashing sound of porcelain echoed behind me. Didn't have much space to work with; I could feel the edge of the blade and the thorns of the branch cutting and poking me. But I could move. And if I could move . . . so would he.

With a yell I strained forward against the back of the robe, and the Praetarc jerked back as the robe pulled against his neck. Choking and sputtering, unable to cry out, he dropped the ball of light and dagger as I felt him scrabbling at his neck, trying to unfasten the robe. I paid no attention, wading forward like I was moving through quicksand, step by step, to the only other piece of art in the room. I lurched to the front of the statue, and there was only one other thing left to do.

"Rat," the Praetarc gurgled, pulling uselessly at his collar, "ver . . . min."

"No, love," I whispered. "The only filthy thing to take down here . . . is you." And with a last effort which felt like I was ripping my body in half, I pulled the robe and the Praetarc down onto the statue, shifting into the locket hanging from the necklace around its neck.

There was a terrible metallic crash, the sound of stone breaking. And then silence, silence like the dust settling over us as we lay on the ground. Ears ringing, head still pounding, I shifted from the locket into the room, almost falling over in exhaustion. The gallery was destroyed, a ruin of stone and canvas and paint. And there, on the ground at my feet, was the necklace, the smashed bits of the child's statue . . . and the body of the Praetarc. Nothing in it now, of course. What was left of his soul was inside the jagged pieces of rock that used to be the perfect, beautiful image of his child.

Jagged rocks for a jagged soul, I thought. *About right, love.*

I heard the sound of footsteps running, voices calling, and I picked up the necklace from the ground and secured it inside my cloak. I staggered to the window, and with my last remaining strength, and shifts from the decorative badge outside the window to the gargoyles on the corners of the building to the corner of the street below, I was gone.

———

Two days later I was still weak, barely able to shift from one painting to the next in my own place . . . but I'd grown strong enough to smell when the woman returned, and to be ready for her. She was dressed the same way as when she first came, and she entered my home even more slowly than the first time. She reached the center of the room, squinting in the dim light, and waited for a moment. "I have come back," she called out, voice sounding strained and ragged; I figured she'd heard at least some of the news. "I have come back, even though there may not be a reason." She took a deep breath. "You killed him, didn't you? I didn't tell you to do that. I didn't tell you to hurt him at all."

"No, you didn't love," I said from my comfortable night landscape, trying to keep the hoarse tiredness out of my voice. "And I didn't actually mean to . . . I was kind of forced, in the end. Truth is, he did most of it himself. I just . . . helped him along, you might say."

She swallowed and nodded. "And the necklace?"

I brought up the lights on a pedestal I'd recently added, on the top of which was a velvet-covered stand. And lying on the stand . . .

She took a quick, shallow breath, and in a moment she was next to it. There she stood, staring down at the stand as minutes passed. "This . . . is real?" she finally asked, her question a prayer.

I snorted. "It better be. Ain't nothing else to find at the Praetarc's now, and I ain't going back there again for love nor coin."

Slowly she reached down, and picking up the necklace, she gazed into the locket hanging from it. With her other hand she squeezed its sides, and looked at the picture inside. But I was looking at her face. After a moment she closed her eyes completely, tears spilling from them and down her cheeks. A minute of her silent weeping passed before she opened her eyes again. "I . . ." she started. "Thank you. I am so . . . grateful. You know what this is? Why I wanted it?"

"Yeah," I replied. "Now I know." I hesitated; thoughts were still slow in coming, like they would be for a while longer while I recovered. "Would have done the same thing for mine. If I'd ever had the chance."

The woman took a deep, broken breath. "The rest of your money," she suddenly said, fumbling for her purse. "I have it—"

"Never mind, love," I said, thinking of landscapes and beauty and wild gardens. "Consider it paid. But don't spread that around in Caervaris, mind, or I'll come and steal whatever you've got left, sure as sixes."

She nodded, turned, and walked slowly but gracefully back to the entrance of the room, clutching the necklace. Right as she reached the door, she stopped and turned around. "Would you like to see it?" she asked, holding up the locket. "Would you like to see her?"

I thought about that for a long while. "No, love," I finally answered, remembering. "I know exactly what she's like." And I brought the lights down in the room and leaned back in my painting, watching the twinkling stars in the perpetually dark indigo sky.

⌐──

Gregory A. Wilson is the author of the novels *Grayshade* and *The Third Sign*, the award-winning graphic novel *Icarus*, called "fluent, fresh, and beautiful" by critics, and the 5E adventure and supplement *Tales and Tomes from the Forbidden Library*, along with a variety of short stories, academic articles, and books. He is also Professor of English at St. John's University, where he teaches courses in speculative fiction, creative writing, and Renaissance drama. He is the co-host of the critically acclaimed podcast Speculate!, and under the moniker Arvan Eleron he runs a highly successful TwitchTV channel focused on story and narrative. He lives with his family in a two-hundred-year-old home near the sea in Connecticut; his virtual home is gregoryawilson.com.

Seven Stones to Throw

Jennifer Brozek

Maureen Burton put her tea cup down and decided it was time to get to work. She had procrastinated for too long—not just this morning, but for the entire month. Magical workings were delicate and important things that required an immense amount of attention. In this day and age of *everything* that was going on, that intensity exhausted her.

Then again, with the state of the world as it was, her sort of secret magic was needed more than ever.

Gathering her supplies, she moved her working to the covered and screened-in back porch. It was one of the Pacific Northwest's rare, lovely and warm, near-spring days. Blue skies, fluffy white clouds, verdant plants swaying in a gentle breeze. Spring wasn't quite here yet, but it peeked over the horizon.

Maureen settled the sweater shawl around her shoulders a bit more, then gazed at her tools. A small pile of smooth river rocks sat on a tray next to a pile of paper towels and cotton swabs. Next to the tray was a package of oil-based, multi-surface paint pens in a myriad of colors. She used to use oil paints and brushes, but found that these outdoor paint pens did a much cleaner job and were easier to work with. Also, they dried much faster. By the time she was done with one side, had taken a brief break, and was ready to complete the second, the first side would be dried.

She contemplated the river rocks. Each one had been gathered by hand, washed, and purified. They were now a clean template for today's working. To the outside, mundane eye, she was about to embark on the harmless hobby of rock painting. What she was really doing was gifting magic to the world.

Each rock, painted on both sides, would be imbued with magic needed by the finder. A supernatural nudge in the right direction for both the finder and the world. Something to make everything a little better. She would paint seven stones today. Three mental. Three emotional. One that was both.

Choosing the first stone, Maureen turned it over and over in her hands, feeling its cool smoothness. On one side she painted a brightly colored question mark. On the other was the word, "Question", also in bright colors and a halo effect in gold around it. Holding it up and admiring her work, she thought she would put this one near one of the municipal buildings in downtown Kendrick.

She imagined the person who would find and pick this stone up would be someone who lived life on a treadmill—moving fast, exerting energy, but going nowhere, doing nothing of import for themselves or the world. They would see its colors and word, be attracted to it, pick it up, and then . . . Well, that depended on the person. Put in a bag, on a shelf, maybe even added to another pile of painted rocks. What they did with it didn't matter. The magic, the intent, would have already been imparted.

The second stone, just as smooth as the first was not a perfect oblong. Instead, it had a couple of waves to it, giving the rock a more abstract look. On one side, she drew a set of gears with painstaking precision then colored it in with green before dotting all around the gears in red, as if they were creating something new by working together. On the other side she wrote "Rethink." This was a stone for someone too set in their ways. *Calcified,* she thought. She would put it near one of the smaller hospitals.

Maureen hoped the person who found this stone only needed a gentle push out of their set ways. To realize things could be done differently. To understand that all they'd been trained to do was not the end of it. Long-term doctors and nurses were often this sort of person. They were people who knew the rules so well they didn't realize that there was more than the rules to life. *Color outside the lines,* she thought as she put it aside and took a breath to reset herself and her intentions.

The third stone was almost a perfect circle with a gentle bulge in the middle. It was almost too perfect to not be handmade, but Maureen knew it was one of nature's products. On one side she scripted the word "Verify" in white paint with no embellishments. On the other side, she drew an exclamation point and put multiple parenthesis on either side. Again, she only used white paint. Its starkness made it beautiful. This rock she would put near—or inside—one of the local coffee shops.

The person who needed this stone was the type who believed whatever they heard and spread it as gospel without checking the source, the fact, the story. That was how mobs were created—online and in person—and how misinformation was spread. She hoped that the simple beauty of the painted rock would entice the finder to put the stone on their desk or some place they would see it every day and feel its message.

Three mental stones painted. Maureen sighed, already feeling the exhaustion of imbuing magic into material objects. While she was no spring chicken, she didn't feel like she was over sixty years old. At least, not mentally. The body, that was another subject that she would not dwell on . . . at least, not right now.

She sipped her tea, grimacing at its cool temperature. It was time to shift to water then get back to work. As tiring as it was, she already felt better, more in tune with the world and doing her small, secret part to make it better.

Back to work, Maureen picked up the fourth stone. It was large and inviting. Its weight begged you to toss it up and down. Or to throw it—for good or ill. On this stone, she wrote the word "Give" in big, bulbous, pink letters and surrounded the word with tiny yellow flowers. On the other side, she drew a bright package with a large red bow. The gift sat on something that could be the ground, a counter, a table, or a chair. It was left to the finder's imagination. She would place this one near a local bank. It might be a bit too much on the nose, but Maureen didn't care.

The person who found this piece of magic was the type who thought about themself first and foremost before they thought about anyone else. They had all they would ever need and wanted more. The magic would turn this a little. Make it more of a joy to give than receive. To appreciate the pleasure of another's need met. To understand that they could touch the world in wonderful, beautiful ways and that would make their lives so much richer for it.

The fifth stone was the lightest and the flattest of the bunch she worked with today. In contrast, it was the hardest of the magics to imbue. It's why she didn't leave it until last. On one side, she drew a shining gold lightbulb with a silver question mark at its center. She complimented this with wavy lines radiating out from the lightbulb. On the other side, she printed the word "Consider" in childlike block lettering and bordered it with solid lines above and below. A faint, thin, dashed line split the word horizontally. This one she thought she would leave in a park. Or perhaps a grocery store.

She hoped the person who found this stone would be young with a young person's energy and spark. The need was for them to realize that there were people beyond their personal world that needed more than they had. The intent was for the finder to understand that everyone had their own world, their own lives, their own experiences. Once they considered others, they could expand their worlds into something generous and fulfilling, then create a lifetime of joy.

The sixth stone, almost as flat as the previous one was a long slender oblong. She knew what magic this stone was destined for the moment she uncovered it. On the first side, she scripted the word

"Empathize" in purple and haloed the word in lavender. On the second side, she drew a pair of hands clasped with a pair of hearts on either side. This was a stone for one of the schools or local playgrounds.

With luck, the finder would be a spoiled child, charmed by the stone's interesting shape and attractive coloring. Let them understand there was magic within it. Let them look from it to the others around them and feel as others did. To know when they did something that hurt another, they hurt themself, too. To feel joy when another felt joy, and not jealousy. To connect with others and know the world owed them nothing, but what they put into the world they got back.

Three emotional stones done. One stone left. Maureen sat back and stared at it. By now, her back had begun to ache and her hands trembled from fatigue. Closing her eyes, she wondered if she could stop for today and come back tomorrow. *You already know the answer to that one, dear girl,* she thought to herself. *If you stop now, that last stone will remain unfinished. Come on. Stretch, then push through.*

Smiling at her mental voice—which sounded so much like her mother's—she did as she told herself to do.

The seventh stone, cool and smooth, perfect for holding in the hand or for skipping across a still pond, waited for its magic. Maureen hesitated. She knew the word, but she struggled with what symbol to use. She needed both for the magic to work.

After a few silent moments, she decided that the first image that came to mind when she turned over the stone would be the one she used. The decision made, she printed the word "understand" in all small letters in neat blue script and surrounded the word with a double-lined orange box. It felt right. She turned the stone over and the perfect image came to mind: a small red heart, cupped in an offering hand. Nothing more. Nothing less. Empathy and knowledge, interpretation and intent. It was all there. She smiled. This bit of magic, she would leave wherever the urge struck her tomorrow, when she cast her magic into a world that craved it.

She did not know who needed this stone. It was both mental and emotional. To understand something was to know it. To understand a person was to know them as well. This was a stone of interpretation and communication of intent—something the world needed. Too many misunderstood small gestures and unintended actions. *We are the heroes of our own story*, Maureen thought. *Let this stone allow the one who needs it most to understand that everyone is the hero of their own story, too.*

Putting the stone down, she sighed with the fatigue, relief, and satisfaction of a good day's work done. All that was left to do was clean up then rest. She could manage that much. In the back of her mind, she felt the magic in the stones. They were all interconnected in different ways. It made her wonder if, someday, they would bring their finders together. "Wouldn't that be a sight?" she murmured.

As she cleaned up her work area, putting the paints away and feeling every ache in her body, she heard someone open the side gate. Perplexed, Maureen called out, "Hello?"

"You weren't answering your door, so I figured you were out here," Felicia Care, fellow witch and one of Maureen's best friends, called. Not that Felicia would admit such aloud.

Waiting for Felicia to appear in all her glory—black clothing, salt and pepper curly hair, and suffer no fools attitude—Maureen tried to figure out why Felicia was here. The woman liked her schedules and, she couldn't remember anything being on the schedule for today . . .

Felicia turned the corner, carrying a large basket. "You forgot, didn't you." It was a statement, not a question.

Maureen groaned. As soon as she saw the basket, she remembered. It was Wednesday. Tea time with Felicia. Her turn to cook. "I'm so sorry . . ."

"Meh." Felicia shook her head, dismissing the apology. She looked at the painted rocks with interest. "I knew you were working. I could feel it. I also know how you are when you work. These look interesting. When are you going to distribute them?"

"Tomorrow. Would you like to come?" She thought Felicia would decline, but was pleasantly surprised as her friend nodded.

"Sure, I haven't been on that kind of run in a while." She put the basket down and really looked at the painted stones, but didn't touch them. She knew better. "You *do* do good work. It's just a shame that we have to keep it so quiet."

Maureen tried not to preen at the compliment. "Sometimes it's better to do secret magic. Nudge here and there. Let the magic find the people who need it most."

"Well, enough about the necessity of secret magic. I brought tea and I'm hungry." Felicia hefted the basket, swept past Maureen, and went inside.

Smiling at her friend's back—the woman expressed all her emotions in action—Maureen glanced at the table and the seven magic stones waiting to be cast into the world. Tomorrow. Then every person who found one would be nudged in the right direction whether they felt the magic or not. It was one small way she could make the world a better place. That was all one could strive to do in this lifetime.

Maureen turned and walked into her little home. It wouldn't do to keep her friend waiting. Now, it was time to rest. Tomorrow was another day.

Jennifer Brozek is a multi-talented, award-winning author, editor, and media tie-in writer. She is the author of *Never Let Me Sleep* and *The Last Days of Salton Academy*, both of which were nominated for the Bram Stoker Award. Her BattleTech tie-in novel, *The Nellus Academy Incident*, won a Scribe Award. Her editing work has earned her nominations for the British Fantasy Award, the Bram Stoker Award, and the Hugo Award. She won the Australian Shadows Award for the *Grants Pass* anthology, co-edited with Amanda Pillar. Jennifer's short form work has appeared in *Daily Science Fiction*, *Uncanny Magazine*, and in anthologies set in the worlds of Valdemar, Shadowrun, V-Wars, Masters of Orion, and Predator.

Jennifer has been a freelance author and editor for over fifteen years after leaving a high paying tech job, and she has never been happier. She keeps a tight schedule on her writing and editing projects and somehow manages to find time to volunteer for several professional writing organizations such as SFWA, HWA, and IAMTW. She shares her husband, Jeff, with several cats and often uses him as a sounding board for her story ideas. Visit Jennifer's worlds at jenniferbrozek.com.

Acknowledgments

Authors have always had a place at Origins Game Fair. **GAMA** would like to thank Gregory A. Wilson and Aaron Rosenberg for their invaluable assistance in overseeing and scheduling the Authors Alcove program this year. Likewise, our thanks goes out to E.D.E. Bell and the participating authors, without whose work there would be no anthology, and to Events Coordinator Cynthia Tuck and Executive Director John Stacy. Thanks is also due to Charles Urbach for the magnificent cover for this year's volume.

GAMA is the Game Manufacturers Association, the sponsoring organization for the Origins Game Fair and GAMA Trade Show. Its mission is to be an advocate for gaming on all levels. To learn more, please visit gama.org.

Atthis Arts would like to thank GAMA, Origins Game Fair, Gregory A. Wilson, Aaron Rosenberg, and the participating authors for trusting us with this project. We are so proud to share these stories with the world.

And most of all, our thanks to you, for reading them.
For more, visit atthisarts.com.

Content Notes

The content of this anthology is intended for adults and teens and is generally non-graphic. Specific notes for each story follow. These may reveal elements of the plot, and are intended for readers looking to avoid specific elements (at that time, or in general) prior to reading the stories.

Pages 1-8 (Art Holds Our Broken Hearts Together)
     War and sadness to children, death of family, suicide

Pages 9-21 (Catharsis)
     Religious oppression, policing, imprisonment, off-page torture, expressions of agony, bodily fluids

Pages 23-29 (ARTBOT)
     Off-page death of child, parental expectations, arachnid reference, blood

Pages 30-40 (Art In)
     Cultural theft, moments of alarm, parental expectations

Pages 42-49 (Shattered)
     Broken glass, a cut and blood, yearning

Page 50-58 (Flower Girl)
     War and sadness to a child, loss of parent, off-page blood and death

Pages 60-77 (Opening Night)
     White supremacy, terrorism, killing, flu epidemic, gunfire, peril

Pages 78-86 (Gallery)
     Misogyny, transmisogyny, rape, off-page habitual rape including children, classism, ableism, off-page torture